FUN CAMPFIRE STORIES ANTHOLOGY

John Bradshaw

FUN CAMPFIRE STORIES ANTHOLOGY

John Bradshaw's website; www.eaglewingsbradshaw.com
John's other published works; Fun Campfire Stories and Fun Campfire Ghost Stories

Printed in the United States of America

·First Printing: 2009 Eagle Wings Publishing

ISBN-978-0-557-18835-2

Eagle Wings Publications

Dedicated to my wife
Alicia

FUN CAMPFIRE STORIES ANTHOLOGY

.

Contents

Before we get started

FUN CAMPFIRE STORIES ANTHOLOGY is a fantastic collection of 46 short campfire style stories compiled from FUN CAMPFIRE GHOST STORIES and FUN CAMPFIRE STORIES.

These stories include ghosts, goblins, bats, monsters, vampires, werewolves, lions, bears and so much more. The stories are imagination filled and some have suspenseful story lines, but all end in a funny, non-threatening way making this collection unique. Kids of all ages will enjoy the stories within and still sleep soundly at night.

Story presentation is extremely important to bring the story to life. If you are presenting the story to an audience it is your job to make the listener "see" the action. It is always the best idea to pre-read the story to become familiar with the parts that need inflection or a voice volume or tone change or action. Memorization is always the best way to present the stories. Every detail is not important. Changing location names and other personalization help add to the enjoyment of the story by the audience.

Most of the stories are original, but several are reworks of stories that have been told around campfires in various forms for years. Several stories are always demanded by kids on a campfire outing.

Scary stories are plentiful, now you are armed with a collection of stories that are fun and relieve the stress and nightmares associated with the scary ones.

There is a tremendous amount of enjoyment in telling a campfire story and watching the faces of the listener hanging on every word. As smiles form at the end of a story, be prepared for the inevitable request for another.

Although the stories in this anthology are non–threatening, always be mindful of your audience since some stories do have a suspenseful build up and paint the imagination with images that might frighten younger listeners.

Ok, gather around, listen up, it's time for some campfire stories!

The sound of silence

Mark had just received his driver's license. He was looking forward to going out Friday night with his best friend Christopher and their girlfriends, Julie and Rachel.

Friday finally arrived and Mark rushed home after work. He had it all planned. His dad was going to lend him his old Ford Mustang and he would pick up Christopher and the girls. They were going to get some dinner and go to the new movie in town, The Night of the Zombies. After the movie, Mark thought that maybe they would drive down to the lake and watch the moonlight shine off the lake water.

Mark left the house around six thirty and picked up his friends. They headed down to the Hamburger Hut, parked the car and went inside to get some dinner. After dinner they headed to the theatre to catch the show. The movie was great. There were plenty of screams and blood and guts for two straight hours. After the show, the friends piled back into the Mustang and headed down toward the lake.

Parking at the edge of the lake, the friends talked about the fun - scary parts of the movie. The clouds were building up along with the breeze, making the shadows cast by the moonlight disappear and then reappear as the clouds moved in front of the moon. The girls said it was starting to look spooky outside. Christopher said that he had heard a story about Cliffside drive. He said that according to a friend's, cousin's uncle, Cliffside Drive was haunted at night by the ghost of a man that was found hung by the neck from a tree on the lonely dirt road. He said that people driving down the road at night would mysteriously breakdown and there were many reports of an evil presence. Many people, supposedly, had disappeared on that road in the past.

Mark looked at Christopher and said, *"Let's go for a drive."*

Mark started the engine, put the transmission in drive and headed down the road. Julie and Rachel asked where they were going. Mark said; *"You'll see."*

Christopher smiled at Mark has the Mustang turned on to Cliffside Drive. The girls said, *"Come on Mark, this is scary, let's go to the Hamburger Hut for a milkshake."*

Christopher said, *"We'll get there quicker this way."*

The Mustang's headlights moved up and down as the car hit some potholes on the old dirt road. The car's rear window became covered in dust as it bounced down the road. The girls giggled as uncertainty was replaced by the thrill of it.

Suddenly, there was a loud snap and the car spun to the left, coming to a stop in a shallow ditch under a large oak tree along the side of the road.

Mark said, *"Is everybody alright?"*

Everybody was shaken up, but no one was injured. Mark opened the car door, got out and looked under the car. The drive axel was broken. Mark wondered how that could happen. Rachel said, *"What are we going to do now? I'm not going out in the dark!"*

Mark said that he would walk back to the main road and get some help. Christopher would stay with the car and the girls. Mark got out of the car and headed down the road disappearing into the darkness. Christopher told the girls to lock their doors.

After a short while, the girls started complaining to Christopher.

"What if Mark never comes back?"

"We want to go home."

"We told you guys not to come down this road!"

"How come you did not listen to us?"

"We can't stay in this car all night."

"Our parents are going to be worried."

"We're going to get in trouble."

"It's all your fault!"

Finally, Christopher said, *"Shut Up!"*

The girls paused for a few seconds and then continued.

"Why didn't you tell Mark not to come down this road?"

"Why did you tell that scary story?"

"What are we going to do if Mark does not get back?"

The girl's verbal onslaught was interrupted by a brushing sound on the roof of the car. Then the bushes alongside the car started to rustle and shake.

The startled girls started screaming, *"There is something out there."*

"Christopher, there is something out there."

The moonlight danced off the cracked windshield glass, going and coming as the clouds moved across the face of the moon. Swirls of dust were picked up by the breeze, giving the dark lifeless road a creepy feel.

Christopher said, *"I'll be right back"*

"Where are you going, Christopher. Don't leave us alone." Julie screamed.

Christopher opened the door and told Julie to lock it after him.

"No...don't go." Complained the girls as Christopher opened the car door and stepped out. Julie locked the door behind him. The girls could see Christopher slowly moving back toward the rear of the car. Soon he disappeared down into the ditch behind the car.

The girls were silent until they heard the brushing on the car roof and the rustling sound in the bushes again. They started to scream, *"Christopher...Christopher."* Their screams got louder as Christopher appeared at the locked door and started to pound on the window with his fists. *"Let me in...Let me in."* he yelled. Julie unlocked the door and Christopher jumped in locking the door behind him.

For a few seconds, there was silence. Finally, Rachel asked, *"What is it? What did you see? Christopher, tell us!"*

Christopher said nothing. He just stared out the front window and put his index finger of his right hand up to his lips and made a sussssss sound. The girls huddled together and remained silent except for an occasional whimper as the brushing sound on the roof of the car would come and go. Christopher said nothing and just stared straight ahead.

Two hours later, they heard the sound of a car and saw headlights coming down the road toward them. The approaching car slowed and pulled over on the other side of the road. Mark got out along with his father. Christopher unlocked the car door and the girls had a fearful, but relieved look on their faces.

Mark's father said, *"Come on girls, I'll get you guys home."*

Christopher whispered something in Mark's ear and then told the girls not to look back as they got out and went to the other car.

The two girls could not resist, they both looked over their shoulder back at the broken car in the ditch. What they saw they were not prepared for. The tree branches were scraping the top of the car as the breeze blew and the bushes were rustled by cows feeding in the field across the ditch.

Christopher just shrugged his shoulders and said, *"It was the only way to make the noisy badgering go away. Next time, you stay with the girls, Mark."*

Eyes

Summertime is the best time. Logan was having a fantastic time at camp. This had been the first summer that Logan went to camp with a few of his buddies from school. They were all in the same cabin and had just spent their first day shooting a gun at the rifle range, shooting an arrow with a bow at the archery range, riding horses and swimming in the lake. They looked forward to the next two weeks of exciting activities.

The camp was beautiful. Set in the foothills of the Great Smoky Mountains, Camp Carlisle had everything. There were numerous cabins that housed about ten campers each and a counselor. The cabins were scattered amongst the pine trees around a central green yard that stretched down to the private fifteen acre lake. Behind the cabins were numerous activity areas, such as a gym where they played dodge ball, an arts and crafts center where they were going to make lanyards and clay pots and a campfire ring for night activities and campfire stories.

The camp was actually built from an old deserted mining town dating back to the 1860s. The thought of that is cool, Logan said to himself. The first question that comes to mind is; why was the town deserted? Logan's counselor, Randy, said that he would explain it later. When we went horseback riding, the stable guy told us that the stables used to be a train station and the path through the woods that they rode on was the old train track bed.

Anyway, Logan and his friends were back in their cabin getting ready for the dinner bell. They had just returned from the washhouse where they got their showers and were looking forward to a filling meal in the camp cafeteria. Logan's friends were hoping that their evening would include a few ghost stories. Logan said that he had heard some stories were really scary. His friends started to make fun of him saying, *"Logan is afraid of ghost stories."*

"I am not!" Logan responded. *"You mean to tell me that you guys have never heard a story that made you shiver?"*

"No, ghost stories are not real, they are made up," Michael said.

Timmy chimed in, *"We're not afraid of ghost stories. They are all silly. They are fun to hear, but we are not afraid of them."*

Then Michael and Timmy started chanting, *"Logan is afraid...Logan is afraid...Logan is afraid."*

Their taunting was interrupted by the sound of the dinner bell.

After dinner, there was the evening swim just as the sun moved behind the hills. After the swim, the campers proceeded to the council ring where a huge fire roared. There they sang songs, played some games and had a great time. The only thing missing was a ghost story. On the way back to the cabin, Logan's friends made their counselor promise to tell a story after lights-out. They looked at Logan and said, *"We hope it doesn't scare Logan that much."* Logan just shook his head.

Back in the cabin, Logan and his buddies changed into their pjs and climbed under their sheets.

Taps started to play over the loud speaker signaling that it was lights-out time. Randy turned out the cabin lights and said, *"Are you guys really ready for a ghost story...a true ghost story?"*

Michael snickered, *"Yea...right...a true ghost story."*

Randy said that everyone had to be quiet if he was going to tell the story. Silence fell upon the cabin as Randy continued.

"You guys know that this camp was built where there was once an old deserted town, but do you know why it was deserted long ago? Well, there used to be a train that came through town, you guys know the station was where the stables are now. Anyway, the train did not always stop in town, but it would always drop off and pick up the mail. When the train came through town, a man on the train would throw a bag of mail off and grab a bag of mail that was suspended on a hook at the station as it sped by.

One day, the man on the train threw off the mail bag and, just as he was reaching out to grab the mail bag off the hook, a couple of kids went running behind him and bumped the man out a little further. The hook that the mail bag was on caught the man at the side of his head and ripped his eyes out.

The man never forgave the kids for making him blind. The story goes that the man was a hermit in the woods for many years and slowly developed a type of sonar. He would repeat the words - EYES...EYES and anybody who had their eyes open, he could find. At night he would come into town and snatch the eyeballs out of people's heads and try to fit them back into his own eye sockets. In the morning they would find the poor victims, many in their own beds, with their eyes torn out and the eyeballs smashed up in the corner where he threw them after trying to put them in his own head.

The town's people were powerless to stop the slaughter that happened every night, so they deserted the town. Many years later, when the camp was just being built, there were some workmen staying in one of the cabins. Late one dark night, they heard, EYES...EYES...I NEED EYES. All of the workmen were killed, their eyes removed and smashed up in the corner of the cabin, except for one guy, who had become so sacred that he had shut his eyes hard and kept them closed the whole time.

This gave the police a theory that might end up in the capture of this deranged animal. Their plan was to put a couple of policeman in the cabin at night. If EYES came they would shut their eyes tightly. Their theory was that when their eyes were shut the creature's sonar would not work and he would stumble around as a blind man. Then the rest of the police force would charge in from the cabin up the hill and capture the killer.

Late that moonless night, the policemen heard in the distance a voice, - EYES...EYES...I NEED EYES...They remained silent as the sound got closer, EYES...EYES...I NEED EYES... Within moments the sound was in the cabin, - EYES...EYES...I NEED EYES. The policeman closed their eyes and kept them closed as the monster started to stumble around the cabin. The rest of the police force rushed down the hill from their hiding place and ordered the dark figure to stop, but the creature ran out the back door towards the woods. The policemen drew their weapons and fired.

The next morning all they found was some globs of green blood heading off into the thick woods."

"Is that a true story?" Michael asked.

"So they say," was Randy's response.

Randy said that he had to go to the counselor's lodge for a few minutes and instructed the campers to stay quite and go to sleep.

Wow, that was a good story, Logan thought. Just as Randy left the cabin, Logan remembered that he had not brushed his teeth so he quietly got up and went to the washhouse. The lights over the water basins had a lot of bugs flying around them. Just as Logan finished brushing his teeth, he felt a stinging pain on his right arm. He looked down just in time to see a bee fly away. It had left it's stinger in Logan's arm. Logan pulled it out and, remembering his first aid class, knew that if he got some ice on it quickly it would not hurt as much.

As he got closer to his cabin he called out, ICE...ICE...I NEED ICE. As he opened the door to the cabin he yelled out again, - ICE...ICE...I NEED ICE. As Logan turned on the cabin light, he heard screams like little girls would make and his buddies, Michael and Timmy, shivering under their sheets with their eyes tightly clenched shut.

"Look who never gets scared!" Logan said, pointing at Michael and Timmy.

The prized possession

One evening, I was driving home from a camping trip in the mountains and my truck started shuttering. Luckily, there was a farm up ahead so I pulled in and stopped. I knocked on the door and asked the farmer if I could use his phone to call for help. Unfortunately, he didn't have a phone way out there. He said I could spend the night in his barn and use his tools to fix my truck in the morning. He even invited me to have dinner before turning in for the night. We had a nice dinner of steak, potatoes, beans and salad.

After dinner the farmer showed me to the barn so I could lay out my sleeping bag on the straw. It was a real nice barn and I was sure I'd get a good night's sleep. Over on the side of the barn was a huge solid steel door. I thought that this was out of place since I had never seen a barn with a steel door let alone one with a door the size of this one. The farmer told me that was where he kept his most prized possession. Just as he was about to leave he turned and asked if I would like to see what was behind the door. Always curious, I said, "*Why sure.*"

We walked over to the huge medal door and the farmer, after removing a steel wedge from under the door, grabbed the iron ring on the door and pulled it open - creeeeeeeek. There I saw stairs heading down into the dark and I followed the farmer down the stairs - squeek, squeek, squeek.

At the bottom of the stairs there was a large oak door with an iron bolt. The farmer pushed the bolt across - clunk - and pulled the door open - creeeeeeek - and walked through.

Down a narrow, dark tunnel we encountered another steel door with a solid crossbar holding it closed. The farmer lifted the crossbar - groooooan - and struggled to pull the door open – uuumph - and we walked on.

A few yards further on was a clear door made of Plexiglas 18 inches thick. It had a combination lock and I watched as the farmer opened it - 13-66-6 - click, click, click and then swung the door open - swooooosh.

Past this door was a huge cage made of 3-inch round steal bars. But, that wasn't what caught my attention. What I saw was the huge monster inside the cage. It was gigantic! It was covered with purple fur! And, it was asleep.

The farmer said, *"This is my most prized possession. Very few people have ever seen it. This is my purple gorilla and you've got to promise me, I mean really promise me, that you will NOT touch him!"* Well, I thought that was about the most ridiculous thing I'd ever heard. Of course, I'm not going to touch a gigantic purple gorilla! So I promised him and I thanked him for showing me.

Then, we made our way back to the surface. He closed the glass door - swooosh - and spun the lock - click, click, click. He closed the steel door - uumph, - and lowered the crossbar - groooan. He closed the oak door - creeeeeek - and slid the bolt in place - clunk. We climbed the stairs - squeek, squeek, squeek and then closed the giant steel door placing the wedge under it.

Well, I was tired so I laid out my sleeping bag and 'hit the hay' as the farmer went back to his house. As I laid there smelling the fresh straw, I just couldn't stop thinking about that purple gorilla. What a magnificent creature! I wonder why the farmer didn't want me to touch it. Hmmmm, it was asleep so what harm would come of it?

Finally, my curiosity got the best of me and I couldn't fight it any longer. Sure that the farmer was fast asleep, I jumped up and went over to the giant steel door removed the wedge, grabbed the iron ring on the door, and pulled it open - creeeeeeeek. I went down the stairs - squeek, squeek, squeek. I pushed the bolt on the oak door open - clunk - and pulled the door open - creeeeeeeek - and walked through.

I raised the crossbar on the steel door - groooooooan - and struggled to pull the door open - uuumph - and walked on.

I came to the 18-inch thick Plexiglas door and opened the combination lock - 13-66-6 - click, click, click and then swung the door open - swooooosh.

I walked up to the huge cage made of 3-inch round steal bars and gazed at the purple gorilla that was still fast asleep. After pausing for a second, I reached out my hand and I softly touched his fur.

He immediately jumped up and let out a blood-curdling roar, turning and staring at me with huge, blood-red eyes. His fangs over two feet long were dripping with saliva.

Needless to say, I tore out of there as fast as I could! When I got to the glass door, I could hear the gorilla tearing at the bars of the cage. I turned around in time to see him ripping and bending the bars and forcing his way through.

I closed the glass door - swooosh - and spun the lock - click, click, click - and ran on. Just as I was closing the steel door - uumph - I heard the gorilla hit the glass door and it shattered into thousands of shards of glass. I lowered the crossbar - grooooan - and ran on. I slammed the oak door closed - creeeek - just as the steel door exploded off its hinges. I slid the bolt in place - clunk - and ran as fast as I could up the stairs - squeek, squeek, squeek. Just as I was closing the huge steel door - ker-thump - the oak door disintegrated into pieces no bigger than a toothpick.

I didn't bother to put the wedge under the door - instead I ran to my truck hoping to escape. As I opened my truck's door, the huge steel door flew from its hinges and the huge purple gorilla sprang out into the yard. He saw me as I jumped in the truck and tried to get it started.

I turned the key and could see the gorilla running across the yard toward me. The truck didn't start. I tried again, and this time the engine turned over and came to life.

Just as I was putting the truck in gear, the purple gorilla reached the door, grabbed the handle and ripped the door completely off the truck. I stomped on the gas, the engine raced, but nothing happened - the gorilla had lifted the truck off the ground and I was helpless.

I just knew that I was going to be torn apart, eaten or worse in just a matter of seconds. I thought how foolish I was to disobey the farmer's wishes. As I sat there helplessly, that enormous purple gorilla reached into the cab, stretched out his giant hairy hand towards me, grabbed my arm,

and said, *"Tag, you're it!"*

Directions

The funeral was a somber event. Old man Williams was 96 years old when he died. He was a rich man, but had few friends. He had lived the last forty years of this life in London, England and had only come home to be buried. Few people attended the funeral, but one of the few was old man William's grandson Ted.

Ted was a no nonsense type of guy. He was a man of little humor. The family had not been close and there was certainly no love lost here. Ted had never married or had children and cared little about himself or others. Ted treated people with contempt, as simply a means to get what he wanted.

Old man Williams owned a mansion on Raven Road. It had not been used for over forty years and he used to say that it was haunted by a spirit from long past. Most people thought this story was just an attempt to keep people away from the property. The mansion was old, but still in good repair since old man Williams had employed a caretaker during the day to keep the property up. The caretaker had just quit after old man Williams died a few days earlier.

After the funeral they had the reading of the will and Ted inherited the mansion on Raven Road. Ted had decided to stay at the mansion a couple of days in order to assess its value for sale.

It was late when Ted arrived at the mansion. Unlocking the front door, he stepped into the huge entrance hall. Off this hall were many corridors traveling in multiple directions. Ted went up the grand staircase and went down the hall on the left.

Tired, Ted decided to get to bed, but first he had to find one. The first door on the left was locked, the second door was just a storage closet, the next door on the right was an empty room. After several more doors he found a room with a nice big bed.

Ted changed into his nightclothes, turned down the bed and was just about to get in when he realized that he had not brushed his teeth and needed to use the toilet. Since the mansion was old there were no bathrooms in the bedrooms, so Ted needed to go find one. Ted grabbed the candle and took off down the hall looking for a bathroom. Up one hall and down another he went without success. Ted was getting more and more frustrated when he turned down the hall on the right.

At the far end of the hall Ted saw a faint light that seemed to be moving toward him. As it got closer it got a little brighter and seemed to take on the ghostly appearance of a man.

Ted just stood there motionless with what looked like an impatient look on his face. The ghost now was just a few feet in front of Ted when, in a ghostly voice it said, *"I am the ghost of Raven Mansion and I have been roaming these halls for 100 years."* Ted without hesitation said, *"Good, you must have found the toilet by now...so where is it?"*

The skeleton

The Gault Middle School had been closed for over ten years. Tomorrow it was scheduled for demolition, but today was clean-out day.

John, Alicia, Cindy and Dennis were high school students. They were hired for a weekend job along with others to make one final inspection of the old deserted middle school for any possible items of value to be salvaged before the wrecking ball arrived.

The rumor was that one of its students disappeared from the school just over ten years before, never to be heard of again. In spite of a city wide search, Ben was never located. Some said that he never left the school, but was now part of the building, haunting it forever...or until it was reduced to rubble. Others said that the school was closed because of his disappearance or because it was haunted, but the official reports said that it was closed due to budget concerns.

John, Alicia, Cindy and Dennis spent most of Saturday morning going from one room to the next. They looked in all the corners and in all the closets. There was little of any value found. Some old books, a broken desk or two, and some dilapidated chalkboards, were the greatest finds. One thing that really caught their interest was a scraping on a wall next to a closet door. It said, *"Ben was here."*

How creepy, they thought. *"What if the story was true?"* John said. Dennis said, *"There are no such things as ghosts."* Alicia said, *"Don't you remember those strange sightings of a strange glow at night coming from rooms in the building?"* *"Yea, probably just vandals or vagrants roaming the halls or seeking shelter,"* Cindy said as they moved to a new room.

Dennis opened the door on a small cupboard in the corner of the next room and said, *"Wow, that's really weird...look."* Scratched in the wood on the inside of the cabinet were the words, *"Ben was here."*

Within the next few hours, the group found numerous places, hard to get too places, that had the same inscription, *"Ben was here."* It gave everybody there a strange creepy feeling. Their minds were preoccupied with the thought of Ben and where he might be.

Dennis said, *"What do you think happened to Ben?"*

"I think he was kidnapped by a stranger who took him far away," Cindy responded.

John chimed in, *"I think he was killed and buried in the walls of the school by bullies. I think he wanders the halls at night for his vengeance. I think they closed the school out of fear that the ghost of Ben would do harm to other students...I'm just kidding, BOOO!"*

A nervous laughter came from the group as the setting sun became evident by the rising shadow on the walls. *"One more room left,"* Alicia said. *"Let's get it done and get out of here."*

The last room on the hall was an old broom closet. They opened the door and looked inside.

There was nothing of note, but an old rusty bucket and a broken mop. *"Let's get out of here,"* Dennis said.

"Wait a minute," Cindy said. *"Look at that rug in the back. That might be worth something."*

Alicia pulled the dusty rug out and the group turned to leave when John noticed something on the floor. It looked like the floorboard was cut, but on a closer examination, it appeared to be a door in the floor. It was a trap door of some sort.

"Look at that," John said.

"Open it," Dennis said.

John picked up the broken mop handle and shoved the end under the edge of the trap door. He was able to pull it up enough to get his fingers under it. He threw the lid open quickly, because he did not like the idea if his fingers, unprotected, under that lid.

The lid hit the back of the storage room wall with a thud. Dust blew in all directions. After a minute the dust settled.

An unsettled feeling feel over the group as they saw the words, *"Ben is here,"* scratched into the inside lid of the trap door.

Cindy broke the silence, *"Well who is going to look inside?"*

Dennis said, *"It's your turn Cindy!"*

Cindy slowly stepped toward the opening in the floor. She peered in, but it was still dark. After a few moments, she could see and what see saw caused her to scream and back away from the opening quickly. Her response surprised the others and they became apprehensive.

"It's a skeleton!" Cindy screamed.

Everyone stood motionless for what seemed like an hour. John moved toward the opening and looked in. *"Yep, it's a skeleton alright."*

Alicia and Dennis looked inside the dark hole to see for themselves.

Noticing the clothing, Alicia saw that there was some sort of medal or pin attached to the cloths that hung on the bleached white bones.

John took the medal off the tattered shirt and read the inscription, *"Ben, 1999 Hide and Seek Champion."*

What Mark always wanted

Mark was walking home from school with his best friend David. David was telling Mark about a scary movie he had seen last weekend that had made the hair stand up on the back of his neck and gave him the willies. Mark said that he had seen that movie also, but it did not give him the willies. As a matter of fact, he had never had the "willies" before and would really like to have them.

That night at dinner, Mark told his parents that he had never had the willies and would really like to have them. His dad told him to wait for Halloween and he was sure that Mark would get the willies then.

Halloween came and Mark waited with anticipation of getting the willies. His dad even dressed up as a zombie and jumped out from behind the basement door, but Mark still did not get the willies. As the years went by Mark thought for sure he would never get the willies.

One day, Mark's girlfriend Sara, told him about two witches that lived near the city dump in an old dilapidated house with a rusty roof. Sara said that the witches were identical twins and that one was good and one was evil. *"The evil one should be able to tell you how to get the willies,"* Sara said.

On the weekend, Mark told his parents that he was going camping with David and would be back in a couple of days. When he left his house with his sleeping bag and gear, he headed straight for the dump. He arrived at the witches' house, opened the broken gate, headed up onto the rotting porch and knocked on the cracked front door. The door slowly opened with a *creeeek,* pulling cobwebs from the frame. Mark stepped into the entrance hall. There, at the top of the stairs, was a pair of women, dressed identically in black robes. They had long finger nails, bonny hands, long noses with warts and black pointy hats. The witches pointed their long fingers at Mark and in unison asked him what he wanted. Mark said he needed to ask the evil witch a question. The witches, in unison, said that he had to decide which witch to ask the question. If he chose the wrong one, they would be forced by witch law to cook him for dinner. Mark knew he had to choose, but which witch was which? All of a sudden, Mark remembered the Wizard of Oz story and he got an idea. He remembered an old rusty bucket in the front yard and an old well. He said, *"Hold on, I'll be right back."* Mark turned and rushed out the front door and filled up the rusty bucket with old well water. He returned to the front entrance of the house with his bucket full of water. He told the witches that he was going to throw the water on them and he knew that the water would melt the evil witch if she did not tell him what he wanted to know. The witch on the left shook her head and said, *"What do you want?"*

Mark said that he wanted to get the willies. The witches looked at each other with a bewildered look on their faces. Mark told them that he had never had the willies and wanted to have them. The good witch looked at Mark and asked him if he had ever seen a ghost? Mark told her that ghosts were cowards, because they had no guts! The evil witch told Mark that if he did a favor for her than she was sure that he would get the willies.

The witch told Mark about a ghoul that had escaped from their basement. He was last seen in an old overgrown rocky gorge just beyond the old dump. The ghoul was a meat eater and could not be killed. The witches explained that the ghoul did some odd jobs for them at times and they wanted him back. Mark agreed to bring the ghoul home.

Mark headed for the hardware store. He purchased a bear trap, a long chain, some duct tape and some spicy beef jerky.

It was late afternoon when Mark arrived at the edge of the old gorge. He saw a dead end canyon, off the main gorge, that had no way out except the way in. Mark climbed down into the gorge and walked into the dead end canyon dropping pieces of beef jerky along the way. Close to the end of the canyon, Mark set the bear trap on the trail and covered it over with sticks and leaves. He attached the chain to the trap and wrapped the other end around a nearby tree. Mark put out his sleeping bag, started a fire and had his dinner.

About an hour later, Mark could hear something moving up the trail. He decided to make sure the ghoul would know he was there so he started yelling, *"What position does a ghoul play on the soccer team?...The ghoulie."* Then he yelled out, *"Want some ghoul scout cookies?"* and *"You're no ghoul friend of mine!"* Suddenly, the ghoul appeared on the trail about three feet in front of the trap. It stopped and just stared at Mark. Mark noticed that the creature had eight hairy arms. (He could see how this ghoul could be handy working for the witches.) Mark stared back, slowing raising his open hands to the sides of his head. He put the thumbs of his hands up to his ears and started waving his hands as he stuck his tongue out at the ghoul.

The monster's eyes turned blood red and it began to run straight for Mark. CLAP went the bear trap catching the ghouls left leg. The ghoul fell over and hit its head on the tree. Mark saw that this was his chance before the creature regained its senses. He ran over to the ghoul with the duct tape and quickly wrapped up the creatures arms, legs and mouth.

Mark laughed as he finished wrapping up. He remembered an old saying he had heard... *"There are a thousand different things you can do with duct tape."* Well he had just come up with another.

It was the next morning before Mark arrived back at the witches' house. Dragging that big hairy ghoul all night had put Mark in a foul mood. He kicked open the door and pulled the creature into the entrance hall. The witches appeared at the top of the stairs staring in amazement. *"Here is your ghoul, now how about my willies?"* He said.

The witch on the left made an incantation and then threw a fireball toward Mark. Mark rolled to dodge the fireball and ended up right next to the bucket of water he had left the day before. Mark stood up grabbed the bucket and threw the water on the witches. The witches started screaming, smoking and melting. I guess they both were evil, Mark thought to himself. He looked at the ghoul, which appeared to be giggling at the sight of the witches melting down to a pile of gooo.

Mark never gave up! He knew that someday he would get the willies.

Years later he married his girlfriend, Sara. They ended up having triplets, three boys that Mark and Sara named Willie, Willie and Willie. Mark finally got his willies.

Boom! Boom! Boom!

"*What on earth was that?*" Spencer said, as he lay in his bed, not daring to breathe.

Boom! Boom! Boom!

There it was again. It sounded like a loud, dull knocking on the front door.

Boom! Boom! Boom!

It was the end of October and Spencer was just ten years old. His parents had gone to dinner and a movie. *"You are so big now,"* They said. *"You don't need a babysitter anymore."*

I'm all alone, Spencer thought. What if somebody tried to break-in? I'm defenseless.

Boom! Boom! Boom!

For a moment, Spencer felt a sense of relief as he thought that maybe, it was his parents who were knocking at the door. He looked at the clock. It was only 8:34 and was actually far too early because his Mom said that the movie would not be over until 10:00. And, obviously, his parents had a front door key.

But what if they have lost the key? What if they are standing in front of the door and could not get in. Spencer's stomach started to feel quezzy.

"What should I do now?"

He felt totally helpless. Dad had made him promise not to open the door when he was home alone. You could never know who wanted to get in. Maybe it was a drunken tramp or a robber. Or even worse, maybe it was an evil vampire who was creeping through the darkness to fulfill his hunger with fresh blood, he thought as his heart almost skipped a beat.

He kept as quiet as possible so that the monster at the door would not hear him. He listened to the darkness as if he was under a spell.

Spencer's mind turned to the comfortable feeling that his parents might be standing at the locked front door. He could not stay in bed any longer.

Vampire or not, I don't have any other choice but to get up and see who keeps knocking at the door, Spencer concluded. Worrying about his Mom and Dad was worse than the fear of an uninvited visitor.

Spencer crept along on his tiptoes and crawled along the floor to the window which is right next to the door. He slowly pushed the curtain to one side and cautiously looked out through the window. Nothing and no one was there, just the pitch black darkness of the night.

"Phew!" His knees stopped shaking with fear. No reason for panic. There is no one outside and no one wants to do me any harm. He thought as he calmed himself down.

"No vampire, no intruder, but no parents either," He said quietly. *"I would feel better if Mom*

and Dad were home now." Spencer went into the kitchen and got a glass of milk. Milk always helped him sleep better.

Everything is OK. The movie will be over at 10:00 and they will be home in a couple of hours. Whoever knocked on the door was not there anymore. It was probably our neighbor, Mr. Miller or another of his parent's friends, Spencer thought as he headed back to the warmth and security of his bed.

He went back upstairs and climbed into bed. Everything was peacefully as he slowly fell asleep. Spencer slept like a bear until suddenly,

Boom! Boom! Boom!

Oh no! Whoever or whatever wants to get into the house has come back again. Fear engulfed him, sweat formed on his brow and the little hairs on the back of his neck tingled. Spencer hid under the covers shaking. Maybe it was just a dream, he thought. Moments later,

Boom! Boom! Boom!

Spencer worked up the courage to crawl to the bedroom window. He knew he had to be quiet. As he slowly peeked through the window blinds, he was horrified to see two figures in black at the front door.

Boom! Boom! Boom!

Spencer could just stare at the dark figures as they turned and disappeared into the darkness.

Spencer ran to the phone and called his Mom's cell phone, but he just got her voice mail. He realized that she had to turn it off in the movies. What should he do?

Boom! Boom! Boom!

Spencer went back to the window and peeked out. Now there were four or five creepy creatures at the door.

Boom! Boom! Boom!

Spencer ran to the phone and called his neighbor, Mr. Wilson. *"Please answer, please answer the phone,"* Spencer said as the phone rang. *"Hello, this is Mr. Wilson."*

"Mr. Wilson, this is Spencer from next door. I'm at home by myself and there is somebody pounding on my door tiring to get in. I'm scared."

"I'll be right over Spencer. Just hang on for a second."

Boom! Boom! Boom!

"Mr. Wilson, please hurry!"

Spencer went back to the window. He had never felt fear like this before and he did not like it. Suddenly, he saw Mr. Wilson coming up the front path. Spencer ran downstairs as fast as he could to the front door. He unlocked it and as it opened, he almost screamed. Standing in front of him were three menacing monsters. Standing behind the monsters was Mr. Wilson.

"Spencer," he said. *"It's OK, everything is alright. You must have forgotten that it is Halloween."*

Poor Rufus

Rufus lived in a dirt floor shack on the outskirts of town. He never had a job and never wanted one. He was the town derelict. He had dropped out of school in the sixth grade, had lost most of his teeth, his cloths were always dirty and he was always on the lookout for an easy dollar.

One day, a developer came to town who wanted to buy the old Duncan Mansion. The mansion had been vacant for sometime and people said it was haunted. The town council did not want to approve the sale if the house was truly haunted. So the developer proposed that if someone from town stayed in the old mansion all night long than that would prove that the mansion was not haunted and he would then be able to buy the old place. The town council agreed to this plan.

The developer posted flyers and ran an ad in the town paper offering five hundred dollars to anyone who would stay overnight in the old Duncan Mansion. Rufus was the only person to apply for the job. He did not believe the house was haunted, but he did believe that this was an easy way to make five hundred dollars and he wanted it.

On Saturday afternoon the town council, Rufus and the developer meet outside the old mansion. Rufus had his old double barrel shotgun with him. The developer asked Rufus if he had the shotgun for protection. Rufus said, *"Naw...I brought this here shotgun in case anybody tries to cheat me out of my five hundred dollars."*

About nightfall Rufus headed inside the old house. He looked around at the dusty cobwebs, rats scampering across the floor and broken furniture and thought, this was almost like home just a little nicer. This was going to be the easiest money he ever made.

Rufus climbed the creaky stairs and found a bedroom where he planned to spend the night. He put his shotgun down next to the bed and shook the sheets on the bed to get all the bugs and extra dust off. He took his boots off and slid under the covers. He blew out the candle that lit the room and laid there for a few minutes counting that easy money one dollar at a time in his head. He got up to about three hundred and forty eight when he finally fell asleep.

It was about two in the morning when a noise woke Rufus up. He heard a creaking in the old house and the sound of something rustling on the floor. Rufus yelled out, *"Nobody is going to cheat me out of my five hundred dollars!"*

The moonlight barely lit the room through the cracks in the boarded up windows. Suddenly, Rufus heard another creeek and a rustling sound down at the end of his bed. He slowly looked down to the foot of the bed and there, staring at him, was a set of white ghostly eyes. Rufus was startled, but then remembered the shotgun at the side of his bed. He slowly reached to the side of the bed while the ghostly eyes seemed to follow his movement. He grabbed the gun and pointed it at the white ghostly eyes still staring at him from the foot of the bed. As he pulled the hammer back he said, *"You ain't going to cheat me out of my five hundred dollars."* He pulled the trigger and boom the gun went off.

The council members and the developer, along with some other town folks, heard the noise and rushed into the old mansion to see if Rufus needed help.

Later that night, Rufus was in a hospital bed complaining about his being cheated out of the five hundred dollars. A lady, passing in the corridor outside, asked the nurse what had happened to the poor man. The nurse answered, *"He will be fine. He just blew is two big toes clean off with his own shotgun."*

Poor Rufus II

In Blackwater Swamp there was know to exist a colony of strange, lizard like creatures that fed on other animals in the swamp. Occasionally, they would come out of the swamp at night and devour farm animals and unsuspecting pets in the surrounding countryside. These creatures stood like a human, but were much more powerful. They had alligator type teeth and only ate raw red meat.

Over many years, these demon creatures had slowly been killed, one by one, by the farmers that bordered the swamp and by hunters, unsuccessfully tiring to display the creatures for all to see. The creatures were never captured alive and, when they were killed, they dissolved into swamp gunk almost immediately.

Doctors surmised that the creatures might have the cure to swamp fever in their blood and they desperately wanted to capture one of the creatures so they could make a serum that would cure or prevent swamp fever in animals and people.

The creatures had been hunted down until just one was left. If they could capture the last one, than there might be hope for a cure. No one was foolish enough to venture into the swamp and this last creature never left the swamp. They decided that they needed to find a witless man that would take the chance to capture the monster.

They ran an ad in the paper that said they would pay five hundred dollars to anyone that could capture alive the last creature of Blackwater Swamp. Only one person responded to the ad.

Remember Rufus from FUN CAMPFIRE GHOST STORIES? Well, Rufus had just been released from the hospital after blowing off his toes in that haunted house. He had lost out on five hundred dollars so he decided to get it back by doing this job.

If you don't remember, Rufus lived in a dirt floor shack on the outskirts of town. He never had a real job and never wanted one. He was the town derelict. He had dropped out of school in the sixth grade, had lost most of his teeth, his cloths were always dirty and he was always on the lookout for an easy dollar. He had taken a job that would pay five hundred dollars if he stayed in a haunted house overnight. Rufus, blew is toes off with his own shotgun and was not able to complete the job.

Anyway, the doctor's group hired Rufus for the job. Rufus would get five hundred dollars if he captured the creature alive. Once he captured the creature, he was to call the doctor's group on a cell phone that they gave him. The doctor's group would then come and pickup the creature.

Nothing could be easier. Rufus thought. *"No one is going to cheat me out of my five hundred dollars."*

Rufus borrowed a bear trap and some beef jerky from a guy on the other side of town by the name of Mark, who had three sons. Rufus headed off into the swamp with his trap, cell phone, beef jerky and his shotgun.

"No one is going to cheat me out of my five hundred dollars," Rufus said as he set out the trap and put the beef jerky in and around it.

Rufus hid behind an old log for hours swatting mosquitoes and squashing large beetles. All he could think about was the five hundred dollars. Boy…he could live a couple of years off that kind of money.

Early the next morning, Rufus was nodding off to sleep when all of a sudden, SNAP! CLAMP! Rufus jumped up and, to his delight, saw the lizard monster trapped in his trap face down in the swamp. Rufus gleefully started to celebrate. *"Five hundred dollars…five hundred dollars…I'm getting five hundred dollars!"*

Rufus ran over to the creature with a big toothless smile on his face. He stared at the motionless body and his smile slowly turned into a frown. Rufus poked at the creature with his shotgun, but it did not move. He yelled at it, *"Hey, you critter, move. You better not be dead! No one is going to cheat me out of my five hundred dollars!"*

After several minutes of yelling and poking, the creature still did not move. Rufus began to fear that it might be dead so he decided to use the cell phone and get directions from the command center where the doctors eagerly awaited news of a live capture.

Rufus walked a few feet away until he got a good signal and then punched the preprogrammed number and the phone rang. One of the doctors answered. Rufus said that he had captured the creature in a trap, but it was not moving and he thought it might be dead. *"But can I still get my five hundred dollars?"* Rufus said.

The doctor knew that if the creature was dead it would have dissolved into swamp gunk. He asked Rufus if he could see the creature. Rufus said that he had to walk away to get a good signal on the phone and was not able to see the creature from where he was standing.

The doctor said, *"Well first thing we have to do is make sure it's dead."*

"Will do," Rufus said without hesitating as he put the phone down on a log.

"Rufus...Rufus," the doctor called out on the phone. *"Rufus, if it's there, it is alive. RUFUS..."* But Rufus was no longer on the phone.

In the distance, the doctor on the phone heard Rufus say, *"Looks like I'm going to get my five hundred dollars after all."* Then there was a large shotgun blast...BANG!

A few moments later, Rufus got back on the phone and said, *"Ok now what?"*

The old house

This story is designed for story telling

The old house had made noises before, but this was different.

Adam had lived there for many years. The house was old when he bought it and he knew it like a glove. He knew when the temperature change between day and night would cause the old brick to expand and contract causing snaps and groans in the old house. He knew where each creaky floorboard was and he knew which door would moan when it opened or closed. Tonight however, was different. There was something else going on.

Adam returned from work and made himself dinner. After dinner he retired to his comfortable lounge chair next to the fire. The expected rain began to fall outside in the darkness, which made the crackling of the warm fire all that more comfortable. Adam kicked off his shoes and took his favorite book from the nightstand and began to read. It was not long before the sound of the rain on the old house's tin roof and the warm fire brought sleep over him.

THUMP!

Suddenly, Adam was awakened in a startled state by the noise. *"What was that?"* He listened for the sound again, but heard nothing except the rain on the roof. The fire had burned down to a lightly glowing mound of embers. His eyes wandering around the room as he soon discovered the source of the sound. The book he was reading had fallen on the floor from his lap. The comfortable feeling of an explanation caused Adam to relax back into the molded comfort of his recliner.

BANG! THUMP!

Adam's eyes sprung open. The rain was harder now and the flashes of lightning would momentarily light up the room. Another flash and Adam started to count…one thousand one, one thousand two, one thousand three, one thousand and four, BOOM! He knew that counting the time between the flash and the boom could give him an estimate of how far away or how close the lightning was. A count of four meant the lightning was about a mile away. Another flash and…one thousand one, one thousand two, one BOOM! The lightning was now only about a half mile away. It was getting closer.

CREEEK!

Adam knew that sound. It was that floorboard upstairs in the hall that he had walked over so many times. What could have caused it to creek? No one else was in the house or no one else was supposed to be inside the house! That sound only happened if the floorboard had been stepped on. Adam slowly got up from his chair and grabbed the fireplace poker. Since he was in his stocking feet, he made no noise as he slowly climbed the stairs. When he got to the top of the stairs, Adam reached out for the light switch and turned it on. He turned it off and back on. The light would not come on. The storm must have knocked out the electricity. His flashlight was downstairs in the kitchen. Adam slowly backed down the stairs.

In the kitchen, Adam fumbled through the catch-all drawer for the flashlight.

There it was, he thought as he switched it on. Disappointment overwhelmed him has a barely visible yellowish light glowed from the business end and got progressively duller. Dadgumit, the batteries needed to be replaced. Why had he not done that?

FLASH! BANG! THUMP!

The kitchen filled with light for a split second. The deafening sound of the thunder was right with it. The sound was so sharp that Adam instinctively ducked. The storm was right on top of the house now. That thump came from the bedroom above the kitchen. Adam reached for the phone, but it was dead. He grabbed a candle from the catch-all drawer and took a knife from the counter. Adam stuck the wick of the candle into the embers of the fire and lightly blew until the wick ignited. With the candle and knife, Adam headed upstairs again.

The rain was falling hard now and the sound of it hitting the old house's tin roof was loud. The wind picked up and that old shutter that Adam had planned to fix started to bang against the side of the house. Lightning flashed with the quick response of thunder as Adam made his way slowly down the hall.

CREEEK!

Adam stepped on the loose board. He paused for a moment and then continued toward the bedroom above the kitchen.

FLASH! FLASH! BOOOOM!

The thunder, lightning and wind were at their peak now. He could see the tree out of the window ahead, thrashing against the window pane. The flashes of lightning gave it a menacing look as it moved and cast weird shadows on the hallway wall. Adam's comfortable house was now strangely different. He felt insecure, he felt afraid.

Without warning, there was a large howl of wind and a large wet tree limb broke through the upstairs hall window just ahead of Adam. The rain was blowing in from the broken window as the wet tree limp still moved in the wind as if it was alive.

THUMP! THUMP!

The sound was coming from just beyond the tree. Whatever it was, it was just behind the broken limb. The rain blowing in the window soaked Adam as he slowly moved closer. The cold water, dripping down his face and chest gave him a chill. The wind was causing movement all around. The candle blew out. Adam clutched tight the knife in his hand. He moved closer to the branch in order to peer beyond it.

Adam reached out to part the swaying leaves when, suddenly, he SCREAMED LOUDLY! (At this point, scream loudly and then do and say nothing. Someone will eventually say, *"What happened?"*)

Your response will be: *You would scream too if you stepped on some broken glass in your stocking feet!*

The animal army

I had spent the day getting ready for our camping trip. My Dad and I were heading to Squirrel Hills Camp Grounds and Buster, my dog, was going with us. I had gathered my sleeping bag, canteen, flashlight and comic books into my backpack. Mom packed our food, while Dad loaded the car. As we jumped into the car for the hour trip to the campgrounds, we waved goodbye to Mom as she told Dad not to let me eat too much chocolate before bed. *"Too much sugar before bed can play havoc on your restful sleep,"* she said.

The drive to Squirrel Hills seemed like a short one. As we went down the road passing forests, hills, valleys and creeks, I spotted all sorts of wildlife from the car window. I saw deer in the valley and a bear by the creek---this was going to be the best trip ever!

We pulled into the camping area at Squirrel Hills and parked at our spot. There was hardly anybody else there. Dad said that it was the off season, so we might even have the whole place to ourselves that night.

We set up our tents, gathered firewood and laid out our sleeping bags. I had never seen so many squirrels in one place before. They were running all over, chasing each other and making all sorts of chatter while flicking their tales. They seemed either excited or agitated that we were there. Buster sure that a great time chasing them around.

As the sun started to set behind the tree covered hills, Dad started a fire and we prepared the dinner that Mom packed for us. *"Nothing better than hotdogs and hamburgers cooked over an open fire,"* Dad said.

I ate more than I think I have ever eaten before. I thought that I would never have to eat again. Dad said, *"Ready for desert? Mom has packed us a chocolate cake and some marshmallows and chocolate bars."* I told Dad that I was too full and could not eat another thing.

It was a nice, peaceful evening much like tonight, warm, quiet, but with fog beginning to roll in from the south. Dad, Buster and I sat around the campfire and watched the glowing embers and the flames of the fire take on a life of their own. After a little while, I asked Dad if he knew any ghost stories. He told a story about an escaped convict with a hook for a hand and he also told another story about and army of rabid animals that declared war on people. Both stories were really scary, but I was brave since my Dad and Buster were there. It was getting late and I started thinking about that chocolate cake Mom had packed. Dad said I could have one piece, but I sneaked two pieces. While I was at it, I found the chocolate bars so I threw a few of those in my tent in case I got hungry later.

The moon was high in the sky and the air was getting cooler as the fire died down and Dad said it was time to get a good night's sleep. Buster and I went into my tent and I slid into my sleeping bag. Buster curled up next to me and went right to sleep. I laid there for a few minutes listening to the squirrels rustling the leaves outside and thinking about the stories Dad had told. Suddenly, I remembered the bear I had seen and remembered a camping rule--- Never put food in your tent while out in the woods. So I decided to eat the chocolate bars so that any bear that might wander by would not want to come into the tent to get them.

In a matter of a few minutes I fell asleep.

I was awakened by a loud screech! I listened for a few minutes and I could hear all sorts of movement and noises coming from outside the tent. I reached over to touch Buster, but he was not there! I started to become afraid. I called out, *"DAD."* All of a sudden there was silence. Dad did not respond so I called out again as loud as I could, *"DAAAD."* But there was no answer. I took out my pocket knife opened the blade and crawled out of my sleeping bag toward the tent entrance. Suddenly, the sounds of squirrel chatter and rustling leaves started again.

I opened the flap of my tent and it was dark outside. I reached over and grabbed my flashlight. I turned the light on and flashed it around the camping area, but saw nothing. I thought if only I could get to my Dad's tent everything would be OK.

I crawled out of my tent and, just as I stood up, I heard a noise low to the ground in front of me. I turned my light on and standing there were hundreds of squirrels. They stared at me with their black beady eyes and their white sharp teeth reflecting the light. They slowly circled around me. I was petrified and could not move. I yelled, *"DAAAD!...BUSTER!!!"* Only silence was the response. Then a voice said, *"We have taken care of them...now its time for us to take care of you."* The voice came from the large reddish squirrel directly in front of me. As soon as he said it the other squirrels started flicking their tails and chattering loudly.

"What do you mean?" I said. The large reddish squirrel said that this was their area and that we were the invaders and had to be....eliminated.

Immediately, one of the squirrels ran up to me and sunk its teeth into my leg. I quickly kicked it off while another squirrel jumped for my neck. I ducked and the squirrel when over my head and hit a tree. Another jumped and bit my arm before I was able to turn and sink my pocket knife into it. As it fell to the ground, I picked up a stick from the firewood pile and did my best to fend off the attacking squirrels, but there was just too many of them. They attacked from all sides and no matter how many I struck, they just kept coming. I could see the squirrel leader standing there watching me slowly ware down.

Soon I had little energy left. I was down to my knees, which made it easier for the rabid squirrels to bite and claw me. Finally, I fell down facing the stars when the big reddish squirrel jumped on my chest, its teeth inches from my neck. It said, *"Now it is finished. We have our victory."*

I didn't feel any pain. I could feel one rabid squirrel licking the blood from my hand. It didn't feel too bad. I was slipping away.

In the distance, I could hear my name. Someone was calling me. The voice grew quickly louder. As I forced my eyes open, I saw my Dad kneeling over me. *"Son its time to get up,"* he said.

I sat up and looked around. I was in the tent, it was morning and Buster was licking my hand.

I guess maybe I should have listened to Mom and not eaten all that chocolate right before bed.

The flower lady

Happy Hills Nursing Home was a nice three story retirement complex that housed several hundred people. The top floor was usually reserved for the residents that required the most care. The entire complex was modern, bright and cheery.

Mary Wells was a resident of Happy Hills who also volunteered her time working on the third floor. She would help the nurses with the residents and she would spend time with the more sickly. She was best known as the flower lady because she spent most of her time delivering fresh cut flowers to every room on the third floor. She always said that flowers made her feel better and she loved sharing that feeling with her friends on the top floor.

When Mary was not delivering flowers, she was busy in her little flower garden on the back part of the complex. Mary spent so much time working with and handling flowers that she always smelled like flowers. Folks on the third floor could smell her coming down the hall before she arrived and the sweet smell of flowers stayed in the air long after she left. Everyone was grateful that Mary was there.

One night in January, Mary could not sleep so she decided to go up to the third floor and see if any of the residents were up and wanted company. When she arrived, she noticed some smoke slipping out from under the furnace room door. She opened the door and was immediately confronted with a room on fire. The opening of the door allowed oxygen to rush into the room and fuel the fire. It was too hot to close the door. Mary almost panicked, but then she remembered the residents on the floor. Mary notified the night nurse on duty and pulled the fire alarm. She rushed from room to room helping the residents to the elevator before returning to a new room and doing the same. As she worked to clear the floor, the fire grew and the ceiling was filling with thick dark smoke. She finally got the last resident to the elevator where she and the nurse joined the resident as the elevator doors slowly closed. Just as the doors were about to shut, Mary pushed the open button and told the nurse to go down and she would be right there. The nurse pleaded with Mary to get back on the elevator, but Mary said she had to get something real quick.

The doors to the elevator closed and Mary ran back down the darkening, smoke filled hallway. She got to the nurses station and grabbed the beautiful flower arrangement she had left there earlier that day. She was heading back to the elevator, but the smoke was so heavy that she was having trouble seeing and breathing. By the time she got back to the elevator she was coughing and feeling faint. She pushed the button on the elevator, but because of the fire it had stopped working.

The firemen finally put the fire out saving the rest of the complex, but the third floor had been destroyed and the only fatality was Mary Wells.

Over the next several months the third floor was renovated and was due to open in just a couple of weeks. One night, the night watchman Tim was making his rounds on the deserted third floor when he smelled the aroma of flowers. The smell instantly reminded him of Mary and this gave him pause. He continued his rounds as he thought that his mind was playing tricks on him. Later that night, Tim's partner

Ted returned to the guardhouse after making his rounds, including the third floor. Upon his return he reported to Tim that all was well. Then Ted mentioned the smell of flowers up on the third floor. Tim looked up at him and said, *"What did you say?"*

Ted again said, *"Yea, I was making my rounds on the third floor and it smelled like a flower garden. When I walked by room number seven, I even heard a sound like sisssss. At first I thought that someone was there, but I was all alone."*

A few nights later, Tim headed up to the deserted third floor. The work had been completed and the new Grand Opening of the third floor was only a couple of days away. As the elevator doors opened, the only light on the floor was a few emergency lights. Tim quietly headed down the hallway. Suddenly, Tim stopped in his tracks. Tim got a faint whiff of flowers.

Could it be Mary? He would love to see Mary again, but he was not interested in seeing a ghost. Every ghost he had heard about was scary. Should he tell management? Would they believe him? It sure is dark in here, he thought. Tim pulled his flashlight out from his utility belt and turned it on. He shinned the light down the hall, but saw nothing unusual.

Tim checked out rooms one, two and three. All was normal except the smell of flowers seemed to get stronger. Rooms four and five checked out fine, but just as Tim stepped back into the hallway, he could hear the faint *sissss* sound that Ted said he heard a few nights before. Tim had not heard that sound before. The smell of flowers was even stronger now. Tim shinned his light down the hall toward room six.

Tim slowly moved toward the room in a crouched position. Arriving at the door, he quickly turned the corner and shinned his light from one side of the room to the other.

Everything was normal, but there was the bathroom door which was closed. Tim moved to the bathroom door, slowly placed his hand on the handle, turned it and quickly opened the door. Tim had a feeling of relief as he found nothing unusual. As he headed back to the door to the room, he heard it again, *sissss*. Tim knew the sound came from room seven.

The smell of flowers filled the air. Tim wanted to leave, but he knew that his job required him to find out what was going on. Tim walked along the hallway wall toward room seven. He stopped every couple of feet to listen. Silence was all he heard, but the smell of flowers was the strongest there. Tim turned the corner from the hall into room seven. His flashlight beam moved from side to side of the room searching. Tim's heart was pounding in his chest.

There is something there. He heard it. He could smell it. What was it?

Suddenly, right above his head, Tim heard *sissss*. Tim almost wet his pants. Whatever it was, it was right over him. Tim slowly raised his eyes and slowly followed with the beam steaming from his flashlight.

There it was. Tim could not believe it. The ghost of Mary…was an automatic air freshener mounted on the wall above the door.

The little vampire bat

Once Upon a Time, there was a little vampire bat. His vampire bat buddies called him Radar. Every night Radar would leave his comfy cave and go out to have a little dinner. Now what is it vampire bats like to drink? Oh yes... Blood...Wet Red Blood...ewww. Well one night this little vampire bat came back in very late to his cave. His face was covered in delicious yummy blood! Well, when Radar's hungry buddy bats saw this they said, *"Hey, where did you get all that blood? Your face is covered in it."* Radar looked embarrassed and he said, *"I don't want to talk about it, leave me alone."* *"Aww come on,"* cried the other bats, *"We're hungry and we want to know where you got all that*

scrumptious blood!" But Radar hung firm and said nothing while he slowly cleaned his face dry. His bubby bats persisted, *"Where did you get all that blood? "* Finally the little bat gave in and said, *"Fine, if you must know follow me."*

And so the bats all flew out of the cave into the night air yelling, *"Where did you get the blood?"* The little bat would just sigh, *"Follow me."* They followed him for what seemed like miles and miles the whole while crying out, *"Where did you get the blood on your face? We want some too! Are we there yet? Are we there? Where did you get the blood on your face?"*

Finally, they arrived and the little bat said, *"Do you see that hill over there?"* And they all said, *"Yes, but we want to know where you got the blood on your face?"* And the little bat said, *"And do you see that tree on that hill?"* And all the bats said *"Yes?"*

"Well I didn't and that's how I got the blood all over my face!"

The bronze ghost

Ben was a lonely guy. He stayed to himself and had few friends. As much as he would like to have a girlfriend, he could never work up the courage to ask a lady out on a date. Ben lived in a low rent single room apartment. He made little money as a street cleaner, but he did love ghost stories.

One night, Ben was looking for something to do, so he left his dingy room and walked down the street. It was a nice night so Ben kept walking and walking. After a while, Ben realized that he was walking in a part of town he had never seen before. A cold breeze went down his shirt collar and he looked up at the clouds gathering overhead. He figured that it was time to turn back. Just then, he saw a light that caught his eye. It was a flickering neon light over a storefront in a building where all the other storefronts were boarded up and dark. Ben knew that it was way too late for a store to be open, but he was curious what the store was.

As he moved closer, he could see the light flickering the name, "Wo Fong's Curios and Artifacts." As Ben approached the storefront, he became amazed at the sight of hundreds of different items jammed in the dusty store windows. He pressed his face against the dirty glass and noticed a little old man behind the counter. No, it could not be … but as he turned the door knob, the door opened. Ben walked in and the old man said, *"Welcome to Wo Fong's. Make yourself at home, please browse around and take your time. I am sure you will find something that will interest you."*

Ben spent an hour looking. Most of the things in the store looked as if they had been there a very long time. Look at that! Ben thought as he moved toward a shelving unit at the back of the store. On the bottom shelf was the most fascinating thing he had ever seen. It was a beautiful bronze statue of a ghost. I have to have this, he thought, but do I have enough money? Ben carried the statue up to the counter where the old man was sitting on an old stool.

"How much is this sculpture?" Ben asked.

"Aw...you have found a very special item. Only one like it in the whole world. The sculpture is only ten dollars, but the story behind it will cost you a thousand dollars."

"Forget the story, but here is the ten dollars." Ben said as he handed over the money. He could not believe his luck. He would have paid twice as much for it.

As Ben exited the store, the store lights went off and he could hear the door lock. The wind had picked up and it had become noticeably cooler. It was very dark and the city was silent. Ben started his long walk back to his dingy apartment when, all of a sudden, a strange noise came from the dark alley on the other side of the road. Ben paused for a moment when, out of the darkness, came a shadowy figure making a moaning sound and moving toward Ben. Ben quickened his pace as the ghostly essence followed.

As Ben passed the next side street, a skeleton with ragged clothing, crawled out of the sewer and joined the chase after Ben. Ben started to jog as he heard the moaning and the clacking of bone against the pavement in pursuit. Ben looked over his shoulder and was startled to see that several more ghostly creatures had joined the chase. A ghoulish monster climbed out of a foul smelling dumpster and made a heart stopping growl as it too seemed focused on Ben.

Soon there were at least a dozen ghosts, goblins and other foul creatures following Ben. Ben did not know what to do. He was so frightened that he had lost his way and did not know where he was. All he knew was, as he ran on and on, more horrific beings were coming out of their dark hiding places and chasing after him. He also knew that, sooner or later, he would not be able to run anymore and the mob of supernatural demons would be upon him. If he could just find some help, but there was no one there. Ben was alone, his fate too terrible to think about.

Ben soon found himself running on a road leading out of town. The creatures were slowly getting closer as Ben's energy waned. In the darkness, through the trees, Ben spotted a glowing fire. Maybe someone was there. Maybe it was a campsite. Ben ran as fast as he could toward the fire. Unseen tree branches slapped his face and tore his cloths as he got closer to the fire.

Finally, he emerged from the trees and entered the campsite. The foul monsters were now only a few feet away. What should I do now? he thought. Then Ben had a revelation. He threw the bronze ghost statue into the campfire and ducked behind the tree on his left.

The ghosts, monsters, ghouls and goblins all followed the statue into the fire and were consumed, turning into dark smoke that rose to the tree tops and then dissipated by the breeze.

Ben was exhausted, bruised and battered, but he knew what he must do. It was near dawn when Ben arrived back at the storefront of "Wo Fong's Curios and Artifacts." Unbelievably, the neon light was on and the store was open. Ben stumbled into the store and was greeted by the old man behind the counter.

"I see that you have come back. Perhaps you want the story behind the statue you purchased last night?" The old man said confidently.

"No...forget that." Ben said.

"I want to know if you have any special statues of beautiful women."

The dare

S pencer, Adam and Christopher were having lunch at school when they started to share some scary stories they knew.

"My dad's friend walked into the Crown Cemetery one night and at midnight the hand of a skeleton reached up out of the ground and grabbed his leg," Spencer said, as he ate his sandwich.

"So, what happened?" Christopher said.

"He was pulled down under the dirt and died for lack of air," Spenser answered, while munching on a carrot stick.

"Oh come on," Adam said. *"I've seen that one in a movie somewhere before."*

"No really, I think it's a true story," Spencer said. *"If you don't believe me than I dare you to stick a knife in the ground on top of a grave at midnight tonight and leave it there. Christopher and I will look for the knife the next morning proving you were there."*

"No sweat," Adam said, as the friends headed for their next class.

That night, Adam arrived at the gate of the cemetery. The hairs on the back of his neck stood up as a cold breeze rushed by him. He walked in and shortly found a new grave. He took the pocket knife out of his jacket pocket and opened the blade. He wanted to leave right then, but he knew that his friends would make fun of him, so he decided to get this done as quickly as possible and get out of there.

Adam squatted down, closed his eyes, and jammed the knife into the ground.

As he quickly went to stand up there was a tug on his jacket. He tried harder to stand up and realized that something was holding on to his jacket and pulling him down. He screamed as hard and long as he could and then fainted.

The next morning, Spencer and Christopher found Adam fast asleep on top of the grave. They woke Adam up and, without rising, Adam told them the story. They looked down at his jacket and all three of them started laughing out loud. The corner of Adam's jacket was pinned to the ground by the knife that he had accidentally run through it the night before.

The coffin

Jim had just arrived home from the war. Things had been so exciting during combat that being home was somewhat a bore. He was looking for something exciting to do when an old friend of his called him up and asked him to stop by for a visit. Jim looked forward to seeing Sam since he was an old high school friend that he had not seen in years.

Jim arrived at Sam's house and the two old friends spent several hours catching up on what each other had been doing over the years. Sam was surprised to learn the Jim was a highly trained Special Forces soldier and that he had been involved in many high risk missions during the war. Sam, on the other hand, had gone into real estate management.

After hearing what Jim had done during the war and the type of dangerous operations he had been involved in, Sam thought that Jim just might be the guy to take care of a problem that he had. Sam asked Jim if he might be interested in a job that would pay very well and put his expertise to use. Jim indicated that he would like to hear more.

There once was a man named Matthews who had some very shady business dealings that had caused a lot of people, who invested money in his business, to lose everything. Matthews had made a lot of enemies, but he did not seem to care. One morning, Sam said, Matthews and his entire family were found brutally murdered in their house. No one was ever tried or arrested for the murders. Most people thought it was probably someone that Matthews had cheated and no one cared about what had happened to Matthews.

A short time later, the Matthew's house was put on the market and sold. The couple who bought it went missing a day after moving in, never to be heard of again. The house sat vacant for many years when a man passing through the area had taken a shortcut through the old Matthew's property. He turned up missing and was found in the woods a few days later. The man was out of his mind, unable to talk and was committed to the hospital of the insane. He is still there today and has never uttered a word about what happened to him the night he disappeared at the

Matthew's place. Finally, a man purchased the house to fix up and resale. He has never been seen since. Several years later, the court give me the responsibility to sell the house, Sam said, but I have had no luck since everybody is afraid of the house and think it contains the evil spirit of Matthews. *"If I don't take care of the ghost, than I can't sell the house,"* Sam said.

"Well where do I come in?" Jim said. Sam told him that if he was able to spend the night in the old house and nothing happened, then the spell on the place would be broken and people would not be afraid of the house anymore. If something did happen then Jim's skills were to be put to the test to get rid of whatever it was that was haunting the house. *"Oh...and did I tell you that if you got the job done, I will pay you $10,000 dollars?"* Jim said it was a deal, just let him have a couple of days to get some things together. Sam gave Jim a key to the house and the directions to it as they parted ways.

A couple of days later, Jim arrived at the old house, unlocked the front door and went in. He looked around and besides the dirty tattered drapes, cobwebs, and the occasional mouse, he did not see anything unusual. Jim went into a room toward the back of the house and unzipped the bag of supplies he had. He set out two powerful flashlights, took out his .45 colt hand gun and slapped in the magazine, pulled back the slide and chambered a round. He laid the extra magazine to his gun on an old table that was next to a broken recliner where Jim planned to spend the night, along with a book and some cough medicine. As the sun went down, Jim had his dinner of peanut butter and jelly sandwiches and a sip of coffee from his large thermos.

It was a moonless night so darkness came on fast. All of a sudden, Jim heard a noise upstairs. A thump followed by a bump. Being an unusual sound, Jim grabbed his flashlight and his gun. Another bump followed by another bump upstairs getting closer. Jim turned on his flashlight and aimed the beam toward the entrance of the room which was just across from the stairs. Bump...bump...bump the noise was coming from the stairs. Soon Jim heard a thump as whatever it was hit the bottom of the stairs. Jim raised his gun and pointed it toward the door Bump...Bump...Bump...then BLAST, the door blew open. Moments later, a coffin, wobbling from side to side, came bumping into the room. It was an old coffin moving toward Jim. Jim raised his weapon and fired. The coffin kept moving toward him. Jim fired until his clip was empty, but it had no effect on the approaching coffin. Jim reloaded with his spare magazine and emptied it into the coffin without effect. The coffin was almost within arms reach when Jim threw the gun and one of his flashlights at the coffin which just bounced off. The only thing left to throw was his cough medicine. He threw it and it broke on the coffin and ran down the front of it. All of a sudden the "coffin" stopped.

Our first night in a tent

In a place where a mountain goat might lose its footing, we put our tent up high on a slope. A gust of wind could have blown it from the side of the hill, but we were happy that it stood at all, so we climbed inside. A wet cold seeped out of the ground. It was our first night in a tent. We were 12 years old and we thought everything was as it should be.

As it got darker, the cold gave us goose bumps. The crescent moon peeped out between the forested mountains and, in the fading light, I saw a man walking towards our tent. He was still a long way away. His outline was blurred by the mist that covered the ground.

I became so frightened by the appearance, that for a moment I was unable to move. The wind played a game with the mist and the grass, which swayed in the moonlight and changed shape.

The man soon seemed to change into a giant bear which stood and stared at our tent. Then it seemed to change into a little evil gremlin which silently crept towards us.

I finally managed to utter the name of my friend. *"Jason, I see something!"* Jason thought that I had had a nightmare. *"Where?"* He said as he rolled over and looked outside.

"I don't see anything," he said, obviously relieved.

His calmness seemed to be catching. Maybe the whole thing was just a bad dream?

I looked out again and there the creature stood, threateningly. I tensed up again.

"He's coming! Can't you see him, Jason?" I whispered. Jason peeked out attentively in the same

direction. A bolt of fear shook through his body and I knew that he had seen the evil gremlin too. *"He's coming towards us!"* Jason said in a low voice.

"Be quiet! Maybe he will walk by us if he doesn't hear us!" We stared so long that our eyes started to water. It seemed like hours that the thing stood in the same spot. Then it gradually moved two or three steps closer.

The moon faded. The first sleepy bird twitter came out of the valley and the sky hung over the slope with a mild light. The gremlin slowly bent over and a large drop of water fell from its nose. I stared wildly at the creature for several more stained minutes as the light brightened the hill slope.

As detail became more defined in the light, we discovered that our creature was actually a tall clump of grass about ten feet from our tent. Jason and I crawled out of the tent and stomped on the clump of grass that kept us awake all night. We had survived our first night in a tent!

Did you smell that?

Daniel and I had just gotten into our tent when the rain got heavier. Luckily, we had just finished hearing ghost stories around the fire minutes before. This has been the best summer yet at camp! Daniel and I had become best friends and I liked every one in our cabin. Our counselor, Bob, was a college student and was a really good guy.

This was our first cabin overnight camping trip. Even though our camping spot was just on the other side of the lake, walking the path through the tall pine trees made you feel like you were in the middle of nowhere. We had set up our tents, laid out our sleeping bags and gathered wood for the fire. Bob started the fire and in a short while we were roasting hot dogs on sticks. The baked beans, potato chips and even the carrot sticks tasted great. As a matter of fact, everything tastes great on a camping trip. The best part about dinner was desert. Roasted marshmallows put in between two graham crackers with a piece of milk chocolate, fantastic smores. Bob won the baked bean and marshmallow eating contest.

After dinner we had to clean up and put the garbage up in a tree so animals would not get into it at night. The sun had gone down and it was getting dark so Bob told us to brush our teeth and get ready for ghost stories. I could not wait. I loved a good ghost story. It was like your entire world is wrapped up in the story for as long as it lasts. Fun, Fun, Fun...

We gathered around the campfire, its wavy yellowish light danced off the faces of my cabin mates. Bob threw a couple of more logs on the fire as red embers floated up into the night sky and disappeared. He sat down on a short log turned on end, facing us. The first story that Bob told was about a giant purple gorilla. It was a great story with a great ending and we wanted more. Bob's next story was about a little ghost that was afraid and then the story of a hunted house. It was getting late and you know... there is no sleeping late on a camping trip, so Bob said he had one more story before it was time to sack out.

Bob's last story was about a huge hairy monster known as Big Foot that roamed these woods. It was half man, half ape that did not like anybody coming into its woods. It moved around mostly at night and had a terrible smell like you've never smelled before. This creature stood ten feet tall, strong enough to tear up trees, had long fangs and claws, and did I mention, smelled terrible? The fire was burning down to a pile of glowing embers and darkness was advancing further into our campsite as Bob continued. Last summer, he said, two campers disappeared, believed taken by Big Foot because they went outside their tent after lights out. Their fate to terrible to think about! Bob ended the story and said that he was going to bed because his stomach was upset from eating all those hotdogs, beans and marshmallows. He told all of us to hit the hay and would see us in the morning. The timing was great because it had just started to sprinkle rain.

Anyway, Daniel and I zipped up our sleeping bags and laid there looking at the inside top of our tent. We talked quietly for a few minutes about the stories we had just heard and how they did not scare us. Sleep soon overcame us. Suddenly, I was awakened by a snapping wood sound. I laid there listening. I could tell the rain had stopped and there was just silence and darkness. Then I heard what sounded like somebody or something walking through the campsite. I reached over and shook Daniel until he woke up. He asked what time it was and I said that I had no idea. I told Daniel about what I had heard and we both laid there motionless, straining to hear something, but hoping not to. The silence was broken by the sharp crack of another piece of wood. It had to be something heavy to make that large a snap, I thought. Daniel and I decided that if we could only get over to Bob's tent we would be ok. Daniel and I unzipped our sleeping bags and opened the front flap of our tent. It was really dark and we could not see or hear anything so we moved slowly towards Bob's tent. When we got to Bob's tent we found that the zipper to the front flap was stuck and would not open. We heard the rustling of bushes behind us. We had forgotten our flashlights so all we could do is turn and meet our fate. We could see the bushes moving. It looked like something big was stripping the leaves off. At that moment we were overcome by a horrendous smell. Then, for a moment, there was silence but the horrible smell lingered. Daniel and I looked at each other and, at that moment, remembered the Big Foot ghost story. Sounds of footsteps were heading our way. The footsteps were coming from the bushes. They were getting closer and closer, almost upon us when we yelled *"Boobbb!!"* Suddenly, a bright light shown in our faces that made us close our eyes. Then a voice said, *"What are you guys doing out of your tent?"* To our relief, Daniel and I realized that it was Bob's voice in front of us, but why was he outside his tent walking around making noises in the bushes? Bob explained that eating all those beans, hotdogs and marshmallows the night before had upset his stomach and he was finally able to use the bathroom.

Spell check

Brad and Jeff had a tough week at school. They both had a pop quiz in science and had not done well. Their parents would find out next week when school progress reports were due to go home. They knew that they were doomed to weeks of extra study time and that any fun stuff would be severely curtailed. Since it was Friday night the two boys knew that this might be their only chance to get out and do something fun. They both wanted to see the new horror movie at the theater and they both liked seeing other people get scared so they decided to go to the movies.

The movie was great. All the girls screamed every few minutes and everybody jumped in their seats more than once. All they could talk about, as they left the theater, were the neat scary parts of the movie. As they followed the path home, they were about to pass the old Hollingsworth Cemetery when, just for laughs, the boys dared each other to take the short cut through it.

The old graveyard was a scary place. There were a lot of criminals buried there from the penitentiary just over the hill. They even said that it was haunted by ghosts.

Right in the middle of the dark and creepy cemetery, the boys were startled by a tap-tap-tapping noise coming from the misty shadows. Trembling with fear, they headed towards the noise since there was no way around it and soon found an old man with a hammer and chisel, chipping away at one of the headstones. *"Holy cow, Mister,"* Brad said after catching his breath, *"You scared us half to death -- we thought you were a ghost! What are you doing working here so late at night?"*

"Those fools!" the old man grumbled. *"They misspelled my name!"*

Parkside Road ghost

Parkside Road had a reputation. It was an old county dirt road that was once an old wagon trail through the county. It was always known as a spooky road, because it was a lonely road that few people traveled and it bordered a swamp that generated a heavy fog that would blanket the road at night and early in the morning.

About a month earlier, a rumor started to go around town that a ghost had been spotted on the road. The story was, that a ghost like figure was spotted leaning against the trunk of the huge old oak tree along side the road. The old oak was a well known landmark along the road. It was thought to be several hundred years old and had branches that stretched in all directions. This figure was spotted about nine in the evening by the minister and his wife as they walked along the road after their car broke down coming from church. They reported that the fog was rolling in from the low area so they could not get a good look at this ghostly apparition. They said that the figure did not respond to them when the minister called out a greeting, but just leered at them from the darkness under the giant oak tree. The minister's wife reported that the figure had on a cowboy type hat and appeared to have a broken noose of rope around its neck.

The minister and his wife said that the figure made a menacing movement toward them, so they turned and moved quickly in the opposite direction. When they looked back over their shoulders at the tree, the figure had vanished into the fog.

Some of the town's people thought that it might have been the ghost of a criminal that had been hung from that very tree a hundred years before.

After a couple of weeks, the story subsided until it was brought to life again, when a local farmer was using the road early one morning to take his produce to town. He reported that it was still dark and the fog was heavy, but as his wagon approached the huge oak tree, he saw the ghost with a cowboy hat on rushing out from the bushes at the end of the swamp and disappearing into the darkness under the tree. His horses became spooked and started running down the road. The farmer said that by the time he got them under control again, he had lost half this load.

People speculated that this ghastly ghost was back to take some sort of revenge on lonely travelers along this lonely stretch of road.

Michael lived in a farm house on the south end of Parkside Road. Michael's best friend Jacob lived on the north end of Parkside Road. Michael and Jacob both attended the same middle school and were very familiar with Parkside Road. Their parents had recently told the boys that they were not to travel the road by themselves since all this ghost stuff was going on.

Michael and Jacob talked about the ghost of Parkside Road while they were at school. Michael said that he was not afraid of the ghost. He said that he was mad at the ghost because it prevented him from traveling down the road to Jacob's house. Jacob, on the other hand, seemed to enjoy spreading the story around school and even adding things to it. Jacob told his friends that the ghost was trying to catch a lonely traveler, who would then take the ghost's place in the make shift gallows of the oak tree. Jacob said that he liked the old oak tree and that he had been scouting the place recently for a spot to build a secret clubhouse.

Jacob seemed to enjoy the fear that his classmates showed. Michael was the only one who did not appear to be afraid.

On the next Saturday, Michael begged his parents to let him travel down the road to Jacob's house. He promised that he would return before it got dark. His parents relented, so Michael took off towards Jacob's house. As Michael passed the old oak tree at mid-day, there was nothing menacing about it. He thought how silly everybody was. He had traveled this road a hundred times and had never seen anything more than a few deer, squirrel and an occasional possum. Michael arrived at Jacob's house unscathed and the two boys played the afternoon away. Jacob's Mom asked Michael if he would like to stay for an early dinner and Michael agreed.

At dinner, Jacob started talking about the ghost of Parkside Road. He was hoping that Michael would show some fear, but Michael just said that he was mad this story had ever started. Jacob went over to the coat rack next to the door and put on his father's hat. He looked at Michael like he thought the ghost would and said, *"BOO."* Michael and Jacob laughed until Jacob's Mom said, *"Michael...it's starting to get dark. Let me drive you home."* Michael said that he would rather walk and that his parents said it was ok. Just as Michael was heading out the door, Jacob said he hoped the ghost did not get him and that he had a secret to tell him the next day at church.

Michael started down the road, knowing it was later than he promised his parents. He quickened his pace, hoping to save some time so that his parents would not worry too long. He knew there was a shortcut from Jacob's house on a trail that intersected the road at the old oak tree, but he knew that his parents would be mad at him if he went that way through the swamp. As Michael approached the old oak tree it was dark and the fog was getting heavier. Michael slowed his approach and thought how the old tree was more daunting at night.

A few more steps on the old dusty road and Michael stopped dead in his tracks. It could not be, he thought, but there it was. Michael rubbed his eyes and opening them again was confronted with a sight that made him shiver. There, leaning up against the old oak tree, as the outline of a person...a person with a cowboy hat. It started to move toward Michael.

Thoughts rushed through Michael's head. What was he to do? Before he could decide to run, the figure was moving quicker and almost upon him.

Michael clenched his fists and jumped on the approaching figure. He swung and hit just as fast as he could, then jumped up and ran as fast as he could the rest of the way home. Luckily, his parents were still out so they did not know that he was late. Michael went to his room and, still trying to process what had happened, fell asleep.

It was a beautiful Sunday morning. Michael could not wait to tell Jacob what had happened to him the night before. Jacob and his parents would be there in an hour since the two families always went to church together. Michael decided not to tell his parents, since he was sure he would get in trouble and he also knew that they would not let him go down the road by himself again. Michael ate a big Sunday breakfast and then dressed for church.

Jacob and his family drove into Michael's driveway. When Jacob got out of the car, Michael and his family were shocked to see Jacob's black eyes and bruised face. Michael's Dad said, *"Jacob…what happened to you?"*

Jacob's Mom said that after Michael left their house the night before, Jacob grabbed his Dad's hat and rushed out of the house to catch up to Michael to tell him something. But instead of catching Michael, he had been attacked by the ghost. Jacob had beaten the thing until it vanished. They were proud of their son and knew that the bumps and bruises would heal.

The boys looked at each other and a grin formed on their faces. Michael whispered in Jacob's ear, *"I think I know now the secret you were going to tell me."* They both snickered and Jacob said, *"Yep, that ghost sure took a whooping."*

FUN CAMPFIRE STORIES ANTHOLOGY

Red sloppity lips

A young woman was driving along an old road in the country and had become lost. She was trying to find her way back to a gas station to get directions when she ran out of gas. So she grabbed her gas can and began to walk down the old dirt road. She had been walking for half an hour without seeing a single car, when it began to rain. She pulled her jacket up over her head to help keep the rain away, but it began to rain harder. Then it began to thunder and lightening, so she knew that she must find shelter quickly.

Up ahead she saw an old abandoned house, so he ran onto the porch. Certainly nobody would mind. But the wind began to blow harder and blew the door to the house right open. The wind blew so hard, that it blew the rain onto the porch soaking the woman even more. So she went inside to get out of the rain.

The house was very large and, though it was abandoned, dirty, full of cobwebs and in need of some repair, it kept the woman dry.

All of a sudden, a big gust of wind blew in the door and then back out again, slamming the door shut. The woman tried to open the door, but the rain had caused the door to swell, wedging it in the door frame when it slammed. She could not open it.

Just then, she heard a voice call out *"Do you know what I do with my red sloppity lips and my long green fingers?"* Startled, the woman turned around and as the next lightning bolt illuminated the room for a split second, she saw standing next to the door a large green hairy monster with huge red lips, pointed fangs and gangly legs and arms with very long fingernails. The woman panicked and ran down the hall. The creature followed her.

Again, she heard the monster say, *"Do you know what I do with my red sloppity lips and my long green fingers?"* as it followed her down the hall. The woman, in a panicked fright, ran up a set of stairs at the end of the hall. The creature pursued her getting closer with every step, gooie saliva dripping from its horribly huge red lips.

As the creature was getting closer, she heard it say louder, *"Do you know what I do with my red sloppity lips and my long green fingers?"* The woman ran faster trying to get away from the pursuing creature. At the end of the hall at the top of the stairs, there was a room, so the woman ran into the room closing the door behind her. She heard the creature's loud footsteps coming down the hall getting closer. She quickly looked around the room for a means to escape, but there were no windows in the room only a small closet.

In an instant the bedroom door flew open and again she heard the monster say even louder, *"Do you know what I do with my red sloppity lips and my long green fingers?"* The woman, petrified with fear, tucked herself into a corner of the closet and hid as best as she could.

The closet door sprang opened wide and the huge hairy creature stood before her. The creature looked down at the woman and, after a short pause that seemed like eternity, said in a voice so loud that it hurt the woman's ears, *"Do you know what I do with my red sloppity lips and my long green fingers?"*

The woman shook as she answered with fear in a quiet voice, *"no"*.

The monster smiled and said, *"Then I'll show you."*

BLBLBLBLBLBLBL (Rub your fingers across your lips while you make the "b" sound. Cross your eyes if you can.)

The little ghost that was afraid

In an old rundown deserted house on the edge of town lived a family of ghosts. The Mommy and Daddy ghosts would go out every night and haunt and scare the people in town and those passing through town. You know, that most ghosts have jobs similar to this one.

The little ghost did not like to go out at night, even with the Mommy and Daddy ghosts, because he was afraid of the dark and all the screaming that people did when he was around.

Anyway, one day the people in town came and tore down the old house they lived in so the ghost family had to find a new place to live. There was the old factory that had shut down the year before on the other side of town and there was the old five and dime store that had been vacant for some time downtown. They thought about it and decided that the old five and dime store was the place to call home since it was the oldest building and already had a lot of cobwebs, dust and squeaky doors and floors. This meant that they could move right in and the Mommy ghost would not have to do a lot of decorating.

The very first night in their new home, the Mommy and Daddy ghosts went to work while the little ghost stayed home. The little ghost decided he would look around his new home and do some exploring. He went down the halls at the back of the store and peaked into this old room and that old room. He eventually came to a door that had a sign on it which said MENS ROOM.

The little ghost though, if there are any men in there, I need to scare them out of our new house! So the little ghost floated through the door into the room. When the little ghost's eyes focused, he saw the most horrifying sight. He turned and, frightened past death, rushed out of the room, up the hallway and hid in a corner until the Mommy and Daddy ghosts got home from work around dawn.

The little ghost told the Mommy and Daddy ghosts what had happened to him and said that they must move somewhere else since this place was evidently the home of the most terrifying thing he had ever seen.

The Daddy ghost said, *"Show me,"* so the little ghost started down the hall while pleading with the Daddy ghost not to make him go back into that room. When they arrived at the room with the sign on it the Daddy ghost told the little ghost to wait there while he went in. The Daddy ghost looked around the room and found nothing but a couple of old boxes, a broken sink and toilet, some old newspaper and an old mirror on the wall. Nothing creepy in here, he though to himself.

The Daddy ghost floated out of the room back into the hallway where the little ghost was waiting. *"Did you see it?"* asked the little ghost, *"Did you see it?"* *"NO,"* came the response. *"Now tell me exactly what you saw when you went into that room,"* the Daddy ghost said to the little ghost. Shivering at having to relive that terrifying event, the little ghost, holding back tears, said, *"When I went into the room, I looked around and went up to the mirror. As I looked into the mirror, I SAW IT! It …* (the little ghost was sobbing now)… *it was a Ghost!"*

FUN CAMPFIRE STORIES ANTHOLOGY

The hole

Clyde and Cletus were brothers and the best of friends. They were simple men with simple minds who lived in a pair of singlewide trailers on the outskirts of town. They grew up in a single room farm house and were educated by their mother, who only had a sixth grade education. They had no indoor plumbing and lived off the land. When their mother past away, Clyde and Cletus sold the old homestead and moved into the singlewides near town.

They took odd jobs around town to pass the time and make a little money. Some days they would help out at the church at the end of the town square, sweeping up and empting the garbage. This church had been around for a long time. An old cemetery encircled the church on two sides.

One day, the pastor of the church, Reverend Haskell, asked Clyde if he wanted a job digging a grave. The regular gravedigger was away on family business and Reverend Haskell had a burial ceremony the next morning.

Clyde had never done this type of work before, but he was sure he could help out. Reverend Haskell told Clyde that the hole had to be eight feet deep, three feet wide and six and one half feet long. He told Clyde that there was a shovel in the storage closet.

Clyde told Cletus that he was working at the church graveyard that afternoon and evening. Cletus told Clyde that he had a job cleaning up at the morgue and would not be off until around midnight. Clyde told Cletus to stop by the cemetery, since it was on his way home, and he would walk home with him unless he finished his job earlier.

Clyde got the shovel out of the storage closet and Reverend Haskell pointed to the place to dig. Clyde started to dig, but found the ground to be hard.

He realized that this hole would take some time to dig.

Meantime, Cletus was hard at work at the morgue, cleaning up. As the evening wore on and most of the employees had left for the night, Cletus found it a little creepy working around a bunch of dead bodies.

Clyde was hard at work slowly chipping away at the hard ground as the sun set and darkness approached. Just as it got to dark to see, the full moon shined through the parting clouds making it easier for Clyde to see what he was doing. Clyde continued to work into the night until the moon was overtaken by darkening clouds, making the cemetery pitch black. Clyde realized that he needed a flashlight or lantern or something to see by. He put the shovel down and turned to climb out of the hole he had dug. Suddenly, he realized that the hole was much deeper than he thought and he was unable to grab the edge of the hole even when he jumped. Clyde now knew that he was stuck in the hole until someone came by to help him out.

Just up the street, Cletus was finishing up his work mopping the floor in the morgue. The last employee had left moments before and Cletus was alone with all those dead bodies. Only fifteen minutes left until midnight and I can go home, Cletus thought as he stared at the clock on the wall. This place gives me the creeps, he thought as he looked around the now clean stainless steel tables, tubs, sinks and gadgets around the room. The clean white sheets draped over the now motionless bodies, reminded Cletus of sleeping ghosts.

Cletus looked up at the clock again and it was midnight...time to go. He put his mop back into the sink turned the light out and was glad to pull the locked door shut behind him. He pulled the collar up on his jacket, because the wind had picked up and the night air was cool. The night was very dark and, except for the rustling of tree leaves, the town was as silent as the morgue he was leaving behind. Cletus headed down the street hoping that his brother Clyde would still be at the church so they could walk home together.

Clyde was so tired from digging that he had fallen asleep confident that his brother would be there soon to help him out of the hole.

As Cletus arrived at the church, a shiver went down his spine. It was dark, the wind was unusually chilly for that time of year and the rustling of the leaves gave an eerie feel to this otherwise happy place. Clyde rounded the side of the church and slowly walked into the cemetery. *"I hope Clyde is still here, but I don't see any lights."* Cletus said quietly. Cletus almost walked into a tree it was so dark. He continued walking further into the cemetery when he was startled as a small twig fell down his jacket collar which, for just a second, felt like a finger wrapping itself around his neck. Cletus took another step and it found no ground. Cletus lost his balance and, in an instant, fell head first into a dark pit. Clyde was awakened by the thumping sound. Cletus, shaking his head, stood up and looked up. All he could see were the sides of the hole leading up to the, almost invisible, clouds rushing by. Fear over took him, when he realized he was in the ground, in the cemetery.

Suddenly, a voice said, *"There is no way out."* Cletus, hearing this, jumped ten feet into the air with fright and landed on the edge of the hole. He ran as fast as his legs would carry him out of the cemetery and all the way home, never pausing to look back.

Clyde was shocked that his brother would leave him like that in the hole. He didn't even try to help me out, he thought to himself.

The next morning Reverend Haskell found Clyde and rescued him.

FUN CAMPFIRE STORIES ANTHOLOGY

The ride

Ben had a rule not to hitchhike because he knew that it could be dangerous, but his car was in the repair shop and a terrible thunderstorm was bearing down on him. Ben had just finished working the night shift at the sock factory. It was a very dark night and although he planned on walking home, the lightning bolts streaking through the night sky and the thunder getting louder made him think again. The wind picked up and sheets of blowing rain starting to descend.

Ben decided that, just for tonight, he would break his own rule and try to get a ride home. After several minutes the storm was almost on top of him and because it was late, there seemed to be no cars on the road. Soon the storm became so strong that Ben could hardly see a few feet ahead of himself. Suddenly, he saw a car come toward him in the distance and then stop. Ben, thinking that his prayers had been answered, battled the strong wind and rain the short distance to the waiting car. Without thinking about it, Ben opened the door, got in and closed the door behind him. Only then did he realize that there was nobody behind the wheel!

Suddenly, the car started to move forward very slowly. Ben was startled and did not know what to do. He looked ahead down the road and saw that the car was moving toward dead man's curve. Ben knew that this curve in the road got its name from having claimed many lives. For you see, that on the other side of the curve was a cliff that dropped three hundred feet straight down into an old abandoned rock quarry. Petrified that he was to be dead man's curve next victim, Ben started to pray, begging for his life. He had not come out of shock when, just before the car hit the curve, a hand suddenly appeared through the open driver's side window and moved the steering wheel just enough so the car made the curve and did not plunge over the cliff. Ben, now paralyzed with terror, watched how the hand appeared every time the car was approaching a curve as it moved down the road driverless.

Finally, although terrified, Ben managed to open the door and jump out of the moving car.

Without looking back, Ben ran through the storm all the way into town. Soaking wet, exhausted and in a state of utter shock, the pale, visibly shaken man, walked into a nearby restaurant and ordered a cup of coffee.

Then, still trembling with fright, he started telling everybody in the restaurant about the horrible experience he just went through with the spooky car with no driver and the mysterious hand that kept appearing through the window of the car. Everyone in the restaurant stared in silence and became frightened, listening to his eerie story. Hairs stood on end when they realized that there must be some truth to this creepy tale because he was crying and appeared to be truly disturbed by his ordeal.

About half an hour later, two guys walked into the same restaurant and sat down at the counter. One of the men looked down at the far end of the counter, saw the man who had just told the strange story and said to the other guy with him, *"HEY, THERE'S THE GUY WHO JUMPED OUT OF THE CAR WHILE WE WERE PUSHING IT!"*

Building maintenance

It happened one day at the tallest office building in town. The maintenance man, Fred, did all the repairs in the building. He made sure that the elevators worked, the air conditioning cooled, the heater heated, the toilets flushed and the lights came on.

The office building was home to a very important corporation and the president of the corporation liked Fred, because Fred always let him know what was going on with his building.

On this particular day, Fred was hard at work repairing items on his repair list when he had a fatal heart attack. Everybody was very sad because they all liked Fred. Everybody went to Fred's funeral and wished him farewell.

Back at the office the next day, the president was very busy with a lot of work with pending deadlines.

Fred was dead, but his spirit could not rest because he still had a lot of repairs to do on his repair list.

The president's secretary was on her way to the copy room when all of a sudden she saw a ghost in the hallway. Not knowing that it was Fred's ghost, she went rushing back into the president's office and said to the president, *"Sir, sir there's a ghost in the hallway. What shall I do with him?"* Without looking up from his work the president said, *"Tell him I can't see him."*

The cub scout

When I was young growing up in Orion, I used to go to work with my Granddad who owned a motel in town. As the story goes, this one room in the hotel was haunted. When the hotel was first built a man got into a fight in a bar. He took a tremendous right cross too his left eye and the punch knocked him out. Folks hauled him up to his room to sleep it off, but he never woke up. He was found dead in the room the next morning by the cleaning lady.

Since then, no one was able to stay in the room because of the ghost of the man. One day, a woman needed a room. Granddad said, *"Sorry, mam, I've only got one room left and it's haunted." "I don't believe in that stuff, I'll take it,"* replied the woman.

While preparing for bed, she heard a voice that said, *"I'm the ghost with one black eye."* Scared her half to death! She ran out the front door and was never seen again.

A few months later, a cowboy rented the room. Granddad said it was haunted, but the cowboy said, *"Heck, partner, I rope bulls and eat rattlesnakes. I ain't afeared of no ghost."* But, as he was taking a bath, he heard, *"I'm the ghost with one black eye."*

The cowboy jumped out of the bath and went running naked out of the room, down main street and right out of town never to be seen again.

The room sat vacant for several years until a U.S. Marshall drove into town. He asked Granddad for a room, but all the rooms were taken except for the haunted one. *"That's fine,"* said the Marshall. *"I've killed 21 men, been shot 6 times, stabbed 3 times, and I eat raw meat. No goofy ghost is going to scare me."*

So, the Marshall went up to his room. As soon as he closed the door he heard, *"I'm the ghost with one black eye."* He turned and smashed right through the door, jumped into his car, and drove out of town screaming at the top of his lungs.

A couple years after that, a family was passing through town on a family vacation. Any idea how many rooms were left? NOPE - there were TWO rooms left! But, the mother and father wanted their own room and their young son could have his own. Granddad told them about the ghost, but the boy just said, *"WOW! A REAL GHOST? GREAT!"*

The mom and dad went to their room and the boy opened his up and went in. He took a bath, got ready for bed, and hopped under the covers. Just then, he heard, *"I'm the ghost with one black eye."* The boy hollered back, *"Well, I'm a Cub Scout and you don't scare me! If you don't shut up, you're gonna be the ghost with TWO black eyes!"*

FUN CAMPFIRE STORIES ANTHOLOGY

The viper

Paul was a wealthy retired businessman who lived alone in a large house just out beyond the mall. His wife had died years earlier and they had no children. Paul took great pride in his house and always kept it in impeccable condition. One sunny day, Paul was out in his garden and had a heart attack. The ambulance took him to the hospital as fast as possible, but it was too late.

Paul left his house and belongings to his only living heir, his niece Beth. Paul had only meet Beth a few times as a child. She lived in the next state over in a small run down apartment. Beth also lived alone since she was not married. When Beth found out that she had inherited a large house and money to live in it, she became very excited and looked forward to starting a new life. She packed her few belongings up and moved into her Uncle Paul's house. She looked forward to making it her own.

A couple of nights later, Beth had just finished dinner when the phone rang breaking the silence of the house. She answered the phone with a, *"Hello."* A voice on the other side said, *"I am the Viper and I vill be there tomorrow."* Beth did not know what to think. The Viper would be here tomorrow? Who could that be? Why would he be coming here? She thought maybe it was a wrong number or a prank call. She decided to ignore it and settle in for a good night's sleep.

Beth awoke refreshed and went to the kitchen to make some breakfast. While she was enjoying her second cup of coffee the phone rang. Remembering the strange call from the evening before, Beth answered it hesitantly. The voice on the other end said, *"This is the Viper and I vill be there this afternoon,"* and then hung up.

Beth started to become afraid. Should she call the police? Should she leave the house and take a room at the local hotel? Beth decided to pick some flowers out of the garden and, being such a beautiful day, she became preoccupied and time flew by. It was well after lunch when the phone rang again. Beth thought about not answering it, but decided to anyway. *"Hello,"* she said. The voice on the other end said, *"This is the Viper and I'll be there in less than an hour."*

Beth froze with fear. She hung up the phone and then immediately called the police. After telling the police her story, they said that they would be right out. After hanging up with the police, she felt better and unplugged the phone from the wall.

About fifteen minutes later, there came a knock at the front door. Beth, thinking it was the police, rushed to the door and opened it. There in front of her stood a large unshaven man, his shirt wet with sweat, his long graying hair blowing in the breeze. He had a tool of some sort in one hand and a bucket in the other. Beth's legs almost collapsed under her, thinking that a maniac was about to torture and kill her. The man looked up at her and said, *"I am the viper and I am here to do my monthly vindow vashing and viping."*

A full moon

A paranormal investigative group in the state was called to a haunted house. The homeowners warned the group that the house was haunted by an especially "evil" spirit that enjoyed playing pranks. The team leader of the paranormal society invited a close friend to come along. He was a physicist and amateur paranormal investigator, who everyone called "Doc". Doc believed that there were no such things as ghosts or poltergeists, and that every type of haunting or unusual phenomenon had a reasonable, earthly explanation.

They traveled across the state in three vehicles filled with team members and equipment. Upon arriving at the home, the team immediately started setting up the monitoring equipment as the team leader and his friend, Doc, received a tour of the home from the homeowner.

At one point in the tour, as the three men approach the staircase that led to the second floor, very loud footsteps could be heard on the upstairs landing.

"Is anyone else home?" Doc asked the homeowner.

"No, my wife's at work and we have no kids," the homeowner replied.

Excited to have his first opportunity to confront an alleged ghostly spirit, Doc walked to the bottom of the stairs.

"Come on! You can do better than that you lousy ghost!" Doc yelled up the stairwell.

"Doc, I wouldn't do that if I were you," the paranormal team leader advised. Doc ignored him. Instead, he stepped up onto the bottom step.

"If you're really a ghost, why don't you show us what you can do, you lousy, no-good prankster!" Doc yelled.

At that very moment, his pants flew down around his ankles. The homeowner and the team leader burst into laughter as Doc, terrified, struggled to pull his pants back up. He then stumbled as fast as he could out the front door of the house. He refused to re-enter the house or to talk about the episode ever again. However, the episode went down in the records as one of the most humorous moments the paranormal team had ever witnessed in a haunted home.

A boy's best friend forever

It was a beautiful sunny fall Saturday. The air was crisp with fluffy clouds and the sky was bright blue. My Mom and Dad told me to load up into the car because we were going to take a little ride. We drove for about a half hour when Dad pulled the car into a dusty parking lot. Looking out the window, I could tell it was a big flea market. Dad and Mom said we were just going to look around for a few minutes. I had never been to a flea market before so I looked forward to seeing what was there.

I was having a great time. There were all sorts of booths, with all sorts of stuff that people were trying to sell. We kept moving through the covered sheds when we happened into an area where they were selling pets. There were all sorts of cats and dogs, lizards, birds, turtles, hamsters and such. We stopped at one booth where the man was selling a litter of Labrador puppies. He had two cages with several puppies that were black and chocolate in color in one cage and another cage which housed just one white puppy. I had always wanted a dog. Mom and Dad talked to the man at the booth and then talked to each other and then the next thing I knew the puppy was in my arms and we were heading home.

When we got home, my first job was to name the puppy. What name should I use? I thought about calling him Snow, but then the name Ghost popped into my head. That was the right name, I thought.

Ghost and I grew up together over the years. Every morning we went for walks before school and Ghost was always waiting for me at the door with a wagging tail when I got home. We played ball in the yard and went into the woods in the state park that bordered our property to chase squirrels. Ghost never left my side and even slept on the floor next to my bed.

Our neighbor, Mr. Hamilton, had a big garden and, every once in a while, he would invite Ghost and me over to munch on some fresh produce. Ghost would try anything and liked most things when it came to eating.

Late one summer day, when Mr. Hamilton had invited us over to the garden to pick strawberries, Ghost and I were heading down a row of berry plants when, all of a sudden, Ghost started barking and jumped in front of me just as I was reaching down to pick a particularly large strawberry. Just at that moment, I heard the sound of a rattle and backed up. I realized that Ghost had saved me from being bitten by a large rattlesnake hiding under the strawberry plant. Ghost came over to me and started licking my face while Mr. Hamilton killed the snake with a hoe.

Ghost and I barely ate anything that night, I guessed from all the excitement, so we went upstairs and fell asleep quickly.

The next morning I woke up and got out of bed to take our normal morning walk. Curled up on the floor, Ghost was still sleeping. I called out his name, but he did not move.

The Vet., Dr. Munson, came out of the back to where my Dad and I were waiting. He explained that the rattlesnake had partially bitten Ghost behind his paw where we could not see it and since it was not a full bite, it took some time for the venom to affect him. There was nothing he could do. Ghost was an older dog and his body could not take the poison.

The days went by and I was heart broken. I missed my best friend. I would still take walks after school into the state park just like Ghost and I had done over the years.

About a month later, I went for a walk in the park. It had rained earlier that day and the ground was still wet. I was walking next to the dry gully, when the mossy ground under me gave way and I slid down into the gully, my leg hitting a rock on the way down. When I went to stand up, I realized that my leg was hurt and I was not able to stand. All I could do was lay there.

The sun was heading toward the horizon when in the distance I could hear a voice. At first I could not call out because my leg hurt so much, but finally was able to muster a yell. A voice, much closer now, said, *"Timmy is that you?"* I said, *"Here I am!"* Mr. Hamilton appeared through the bushes and kneeled by my side. He could see that my leg was hurt, so he got up and told me he would be right back. Moments later, Mr. Hamilton returned with two sticks and some vines. He put my hurt leg between the two sticks and wrapped them together with the vine so it would not move. He slowly picked me up and started up the slope of the gully.

As we were approaching my house, Mr. Hamilton said, *"That dog of yours is really something special."* *"What do you mean,"* I responded. Mr. Hamilton said that he was working in his garden when Ghost came running toward him barking and did not stop barking until he followed Ghost into the state park. *"I know that Ghost is always with you so I called your name. When I heard you yell, Ghost ran into the bushes just ahead of me. When I came through the bushes, I found you, but I don't know where Ghost went."*

Dad explained to Mr. Hamilton that Ghost had died a month earlier, but I knew that Ghost was still with me, still looking out for me. My best friend forever!

The fearless one

William was ten years old and had never been afraid of anything. He had heard many ghost stories, had seen many "scary" movies and none had every scared him. Will loved Halloween more than any other holiday. He loved to dress up and scare his friends, but they could never scare him.

This Halloween, his cousin, who lived in the next town over, invited Will to attend a Halloween party with him and then go trick or treating. Will had never been to his cousin's house before and, on top of that, he had heard about a haunted swamp just on the outskirts of the town that he thought would be fun to see.

As Halloween arrived, Will's parents drove him over to his cousin's house to spend the night. At dinner, Will asked about the story of the haunted swamp. Will's cousin told him that the swamp was a place to stay away from on Halloween night because the headless horseman roamed the swamp looking for victims until dawn. No one knew who the headless horseman was, where he came from, why he was there on Halloween or how he got headless. Will said that he would love to see this guy.

As night descended, Will and his cousin changed into their costumes and headed out to the Halloween party on the edge of town. Will dressed up as a warlock and his cousin was Frankenstein. Part of the activities at the party was a haunted house put on by some of the kids. Will's cousin played a part in the haunted house. Will went through the haunted house, but it did not scare him. He knew that his cousin would be in the haunted house for some time so Will decided that this would be his chance to sneak out to the swamp which was just a mile up the road. He would be back before anybody knew he was gone.

Will went out into the night and headed down the road towards the swamp. Will did not see anybody on the way there. Apparently, everybody stayed clear of this area on Halloween. There was a full moon out that made the swamp visible even though there was a mist rising off the damp ground. Will was excited in the hopes of seeing the headless horseman. He walked down the road that bordered the swamp until he found a fairly dry break in the foliage that allowed him the head into the swamp.

The damp fern covered ground barely made a sound as Will walked and walked. The trees took on a look like he had seen last year in a swamp monster movie. Raising out of the swamp water, the trees, hanging with moss, occasionally blocked some of the bright moonlight shinning down through the thickening mist. An owl's howl was the only thing that broke the silence all around him.

Will started to become disappointed since he was really hoping to see the headless horseman. He knew that he was going to have to turn back soon.

Suddenly, in the distance ahead of him, Will heard the cloppity clop sound of a hoofed animal heading toward him. As it got closer, he could hear a snorting sound of an animal breathing hard. Will stood there staining his eyes when, coming out of the mist at a full gallop was a horse snorting mist out of its nose. The rider wore a dark flowing cloak, held the reins with black gloves and appeared to be headless. Will could not believe his eyes. *"How Cool,"* he said. Just as the horse was almost in arms length, a dark cloud moved in front of the moon and darkness fell over the swamp. Will could feel the movement of the air as the horse and rider rushed by.

The cloud moved away from the moon making the swamp visible again. Will remained silent hoping to hear the sound of the running horse, but all was quite. Even the owl's howl had stopped. Moments later, the horse and headless rider appeared from a different direction heading toward Will. Will just stood there and called out, *"WOW this is so cool. I wish my cousin was here to see this!"* The headless horseman came again from another direction and rushed by Will, the horse snorting and hoofs clanking. Will was having such a great time that he sat on the fern covered ground and yelled out into the dark, *"Do it again."*

The horse and headless rider charged again and again, going by Will with just inches to spare. About an hour later the horse and rider made one last charge. Will just sat there clapping. As the horse got closer it started to slow until it finally stopped right next to Will. It just stood there pawing the ground with one leg and breathing hard while the headless rider sat there kind of slumped over like he was tired. Will stood up and said that he enjoyed seeing them, but it was late and he had to get back to the Halloween party. The only thing was that, in all the excitement, he had forgotten the way back. Will thought for a moment and then said, *"Can you give me a ride?"* If a horse can make an expression than it appeared to Will to say, you've got to be kidding me! The horse looked back at the headless rider shook his head once and in a moment the headless rider reached out his gloved hand toward Will. Will grabbed the glove and was pulled up onto the horse. Sitting behind the headless rider, the horse reared up and started running like the wind. Within a couple of minutes the horse stopped just outside of the building where the Halloween party was being held. Will jumped off, thanked the headless horseman and waved as the horse and rider disappeared down the road.

Will rushed into the party and told his cousin and his friends all about it. He even took them outside to show them the hoof marks in the dirt road. They initially did not believe him, but after a few years of no headless horseman sightings, everyone began to believe the story of the boy with no fear. He became known as the only person who could give a headless horseman a headache.

The Old Lady

Frank's house sat across the street from the park. Frank, who was retired, liked to sit on his front porch and watch all the people in the park. Day after day he saw an old lady sitting on the same park bench reading a book.

As the days rolled by, Frank became more and more interested in the old lady and what she was reading. Whatever it was, it must be very interesting.

Frank liked to read and, not being a spring chicken himself, he thought that maybe he could relieve some boredom and make a friend.

He worked up the courage and got up off his porch swing, walked across the road into the park and sat down on the bench next to the old lady. She didn't look up, but just kept reading that interesting looking book.

After a few minutes, Frank asked the old lady, *"What are you reading?"* Without looking up, the old lady said that it was a book of ghost stories. Frank paused for a minute, but wanting to continue the conversation said, *"I wish I could believe in ghosts."* The old lady looked up from her book and stared at Frank with sunken pale eyes and said, *"Oh really? You don't believe in ghosts?"* Suddenly, the old lady vanished in front of Frank's eyes leaving nothing behind except for the book on ghosts. NOW YOU HAVE IT.

Be careful what you wish for, you might just get it!

Jimmy's summer job

Jimmy was out of school on summer break. He was looking for a summer job, but had little success. The job market in the little town of Backwater was crummy. The few summer jobs available were taken by other kids who had the same job the summer before. This was Jimmy's first summer where he was able to work. He had been looking forward to earning some extra money and having something constructive to do during the long summer hours.

One day Jimmy woke up and decided that today would be the day he would find a job. He got up, washed up, dressed nicely, ate a good breakfast and after giving his Mom a kiss, headed out the door. He rode his bike to the hardware store, but no luck...he went to the hamburger joint, but their schedule was filled...he headed to the movie rental place and again no luck. After another couple of stops with no success, his spirits beaten down, Jimmy turned his bike around for the long ride home.

As the hard top road turned into a dirt road the sun was slowly settling toward the western horizon. The old Black Hill Cemetery was just ahead on the left marking the halfway point between town and Jimmy's house.

As Jimmy got closer to the old graveyard he noticed a sign stuck in the ground that he had not seen before today. It said...SUMMER HELP WANTED IMMEDIATELY INQUIRE AT THE GATE. Jimmy slammed on his brakes and stared at the sign. He thought to himself...A JOB! He stared at the old under cared for, overgrown graveyard and thought about how creepy this place was. He assumed it was not used anymore since there never seemed to be any activity around the place and everybody went to the large nicely manicured cemetery on the other side of town. Jimmy walked up to the old rusty gate and called out, *"Is anybody there?"* Silence was the response. Jimmy again called out, *"Is anybody there?"* Turning to leave, a scratchy hoarse voice came from the far side of the gate. *"What do you want?"* Jimmy turned back around and seeing the old bent over man with gray stringy shoulder length hair, almost decided to jump on his bike and take off. Taking a deep breath, he told the old man that he had seen the help wanted sign and was there to see if the job was open.

The old man said that his name was Frank Johnson and that he was the owner of the cemetery. He had been sick for a long time and was not able to keep the place up. He said that people did not want to get buried there anymore because they thought the place was hunted. However, there were still a few unoccupied spaces that had been purchased but unfilled and, as a matter of fact, he had one customer that had to be buried by law before the day was done. He had no equipment except a shovel and he was too weak to do it himself. Mr. Johnson said that if Jimmy wanted the job, he would have to dig a hole six feet deep for his customer. (He pointed to an old pinewood coffin lying on the ground near by.) Jimmy would have to put the coffin in the hole and cover it up by midnight. If Jimmy did that, Mr. Johnson said that he would pay him to clean up the place during the summer.

Jimmy grabbed the shovel and said, *"Where do I dig?"* The old man led Jimmy up a broken path through the overgrown foliage, under giant oak trees to a dark spot towards the center of the cemetery. The old man pointed to the spot and said, *"Funny thing about this customer, his name was Jimmy, just like your name. He first died forty years ago in a farming accident, but just as they were about to cover him up, his eyes opened and he was alive. They thought that he might have been in a comma or something and the doctors mistakenly thought he was dead. He lived a full life until last month when he really did die. His dying wish was to be buried in the same coffin and the same spot used the first time. His last will and testament stated that he did not want to be buried until the last possible day allowed by law and that was today."* Mr. Johnson said that he thought that was because Jimmy was afraid to be buried alive like what almost happened to him years before.

Mr. Johnson said that he did not feel well and so he thought that he would go home. He told Jimmy that since he would be working late that night, to not worry about coming in to work until the day after tomorrow. Mr. Johnson turned and left while Jimmy started to dig.

Jimmy was about three feet down when the sun went down and the shadows of the graveyard turned into darkness. Thank goodness Mr. Johnson had left a lantern to give some light. The air became heavy with dew which turned into a mist rising from the graves. A slight breeze stirred the trees just enough to flicker the lantern light and give movement to the shadows caused by the light.

As eleven o'clock approached, Jimmy had dug down about five feet and the graveyard had become very scary. The breeze made the tree limps sway, rubbing on one another making all sorts of strange sounds. The mist was heavy and the night was very dark. Silent lightning flashed far away and the clouds must have been heavy since there was no star or moonlight. Suddenly, Jimmy remembered that no one knew where he was. I'm sure my Mom is very worried about me, he thought as he quickened his pace.

As eleven thirty arrived Jimmy was about to take the last shovel full of dirt out of the hole when all of a sudden his shovel head hit something hard. Jimmy tried a different spot and it was just as hard. Jimmy brushed the dirt off with his hands to discover, what looked like, the top of a coffin.

At first Jimmy was afraid and he knew he was running out of time. Jimmy noticed that the lid was not nailed shut so he decided to look inside, believing the coffin was empty. Rain started to fall and the lightning was getting closer. The wind picked up. Jimmy reached down putting his fingers under the lid on one side. He slowly pulled the lid up and just as he was about to see inside, a big gust of wind blew the lantern light out. A lightning bolt cracked loudly overhead and............

THAT IS WHY PEOPLE WHO WORK IN CEMETARYS DO NOT LIKE THE GRAVEYARD SHIFT

FUN CAMPFIRE STORIES ANTHOLOGY

Hell's fury

The old lady had just exited the store, purse in hand, when a man rushed up behind her and snatched her purse. The strap broke as the man pulled the purse away and ran through the parking lot and into the trees behind the store. The old lady was knocked over by the event, received a concussion and suffered a broken hip.

Max ran several blocks until he felt safe enough to stop and examine his loot. He propped the purse up on a pile of old tires behind the tire store and opened it up. His take for this effort amounted to twelve dollars and some change. Not what he hoped for, but better than nothing. Max than took his windfall to the drug store. He picked up a pack of gum for fifty cents, handed the young clerk a one dollar bill. When the clerk returned the change of fifty cents, Max complained that he had given the clerk a ten dollar bill and wanted his extra nine dollars in change. After the manager responded to the scene, Max was given the change that was not rightfully his.

Max had lied, cheated, swindled and stolen just about every day of his life. Max thought he was king of the streets, but at home, it was a different matter. Max went to the local bar and drank up all the money he got from the old lady and a couple of dollars his wife had given him.

Max's wife, Bertha, was a very big woman. Max and Bertha had married about five years earlier after Max had a few days of heavy drinking. Max could not even remember where he had met Bertha, but he was definitely afraid of her. Max was not a big guy and Bertha, more than once had laid Max out with a simple left cross. Max would like nothing more than to leave Bertha, but he knew that she would never allow it.

When Max arrived home, Bertha said, *"Where have you been, you no good bum? Did you bring home my cookies, like I told you?"*

"No dear." was the timid response. *"I lost the money, honey."*

Bertha stormed toward Max with her huge fists clenched. She yelled, *"I should stomp you like the insect you are! You are the worst husband, worst provider and stupidest man on the planet. I can't stand you! Did you find a job today, you wretched excuse for a man?"*

"No honey." Max said, expecting to be pummeled at any moment.

Bertha raised her huge right hand and slapped Max on the left side of his face so hard that a red hand print was left on his cheek for a few moments. She then raised the other hand and did the same for the other side of his face. *"You will get this everyday until you find a decent job, you worm scum! Do you understand me?"*

"Yes, my love." came the sobbing response.

"Now get in the kitchen and make me dinner. After dinner you will clean the dishes and get my bath ready. Remember tonight is the night you clean my toenails and drain that boil on my leg!"

After dinner, Max took the trash out to the street. It was dark and Max lived in a bad neighborhood. A man came up to Max and demanded money. Max pulled out a knife and the man shot Max dead.

Next thing Max knew, he was standing at some red gates, guarding the entrance to a fiery red tunnel. He could not go anywhere else. There was smoke all around and it was hot. Soon a red lizard with a long tail and wings appeared at the gate and opened it. *"Follow me."* it said.

Max and the flying lizard headed down the tunnel. There was molten lava seeping from the walls of the tunnel and the smell of sulfur was almost overwhelming, but at least he was not draining Bertha's boil. Soon they arrived at a desk that was engulfed in flames. Behind the desk sat a red skinned, half man, half goat creature that had a long barbed tail and blood red eyes.

"Name please?" The creature said.

"My name is Max."

"Ah yes, your name is on my reservation list. I am THE DEVIL. Now we just have to figure out where in hell you belong. Have you lied and cheated?"

Max tried, but found he was unable to lie to this creature. He confessed that he had lied and cheated. The Devil waved his claw like hand as if to say, follow me. They walked down the tunnel that now had many doors on each side. They came to a door that had a sign on it that said, - Liars and Cheaters. The Devil opened the door and inside Max saw people packed tightly together and all they could do is lie to each other for eternity. The Devil said, *"This is where you belong unless you have stolen."* Max did not want to stay in that room and he could not lie, so he was glad when he had to say, *"Yes I have stolen."*

"Then you can not stay here. Follow me." They moved down to the door marked, Thieves and the Devil opened the door. Inside were even more people packed together tighter than sardines. They were starving because they were stealing each other's food. *"In here you steel and starve for eternity,"* the Devil said. You belong in here unless you have hurt someone on purpose.

Max was glad to say that yes he had hurt people on purpose because he could not tell the creature a lie and he definitely did not want to stay in that room.

The Devil closed the door and said, *"You do not belong in this room. Follow me."*

Down the tunnel the Devil and Max went. The heat was more intense and the smell overwhelming. The sound of people screaming almost made your ears hurt. Soon they came to a door that said, People Who Hurt Other People. The Devil opened the door and inside Max saw more people than he thought could be put into a room. They were all screaming as they spent eternity hurting each other. The Devil said, *"It looks like this is where you belong, Max...unless you have scorned your wife."*

Max was unable to lie. *"Yes, I have. I have cheated on her and lied to her and wanted to leave my wretched life with her."*

The Devil motioned for Max to follow him. They descended even farther into hell. The heat was so bad that all you could do is sweat and burn. The sulfur smell burned your throat and lungs and the screams from this portion of hell were louder and longer than any other. A moment later they exited the tunnel through a back door.

The air was clear and there was no sulfur smell and the heat was gone. Just ahead of them was a beautiful white door. *"You are no longer in hell."* the Devil said. *"You belong in that room,"* as the Devil pointed his claw at the door.

"Is that heaven?" Max asked.

The Devil laughed as he opened the door marked, Scorned Women. Inside was the interior of Max's house and in the room were thousands of

Berthas all screaming at Max, all wanting to be fed, all with festering boils, all with clenched fists. *"Hell has no fury like a woman scorned. Welcome to your eternity, Max."* The Devil sneered.

The last flight

It was the day before Halloween and Matthew was trying to get home. It had been a long week at work away from home. He did not have to travel often for work and for this, he was grateful since Matthew did not like to fly. Most of the time, when he did fly, he was with an associate, but this time was different, he was alone.

Matthew finished his job a day early and he was really hoping to get home to his wife and three kids so he could enjoy Halloween with them. He arrived at the airport hoping to catch an early flight home, but all the flights were booked and all he could do was to wait stand-by.

Unfortunately, he was unable to get a seat on any of the regularly scheduled flights. Matthew stared at the departure board as the last scheduled flight of the day departed. He finally realized that he would have to spend the night there and hope to catch an earlier flight in the morning. The terminal was empty as he glanced one last time at the board. He could not believe his eyes! He looked again, an unscheduled flight showed up on the departure board and departure time was one minute after midnight. Gate thirteen was at the very end of the concourse and midnight was just five minutes away.

Matthew grabbed his carry on bag and sprinted down the concourse. As he arrived at the deserted gate, there was a sign next to the open gate door that said, Welcome Aboard. Excited that he might get home, Matthews ran down the ramp and stepped onto the plane. The door closed behind him by itself.

The airplane was dark with just a slight amount of light coming from the emergency lights. Matthew stood there for a few moments until his eyes adjusted to the dim light.

"Welcome aboard Halloween Airlines." The voice came from a figure standing in front of him.

Matthew stared at the dark figure and could slowly make out some features that made his jaw drop. Standing in front of him was a hideous creature. It was mostly skeletal, but still had some rotting skin loosely hanging on its blood stained bones. It had stringy hair and a tattered flight attendant's outfit on. Matthew saw cobwebs on the walls and ceiling, the carpet under his feet was torn and tattered and there were, what appeared to be, roaches crawling everywhere. Matthew then realized that it was Halloween and that this must be some sort of a theme flight. Well, if it got him home in time to enjoy Halloween with his family, then that was ok with him.

The scary looking figure said, *"Sir, you can take any open seat."* Matthew wondered how they got that thing to look so lifelike. It certainly could not be a costume! He turned and started to follow the emergency isle lights into the interior of the plane. His eyes were adjusting better to the dim light and he was amazed at the things he was seeing. Most of the seats were tattered and bent, the overhead bins were broken or missing, the windows appeared to have cracks in them, the carpet was torn up and there were wires and cobwebs hanging from everywhere. What he saw sitting in the few occupied seats even amazed him more. There were all sorts of strange looking creatures. In one seat there was a werewolf, in another a reptilian type swamp monster. There were skeletons everywhere and cold wispy mists floating throughout the cabin. Boy, this cost some bucks to put together, Matthew thought.

Matthew found a seat that did not have a creature or skeleton next to it and sat down. The intercom system crackled to life followed by an announcement, *"Welcome aboard Halloween Airlines, we are pleased to have some of the best pilots in the industry... Unfortunately, none of them are on this flight...! Not that it will matter, but to operate your seatbelt, insert the metal tab into the buckle, and pull tight. It works just like every other seatbelt, and if you don't know how to operate one, you probably shouldn't be out in public unsupervised at night."* Matthew reached for his seat belt, but found none. This has got to be a joke, he thought.

"In the usual event of a sudden loss of cabin pressure, oxygen masks might descend from the ceiling. Stop screaming, grab the nearest mask too you and pull it over your face. If you have a small child traveling with you, secure your mask first before assisting with theirs. If you are traveling with two or more small children, decide now which one you love the most.

There are no operating emergency exits and since our flight will be over rock hard solid ground you have no need for a flotation device. In the seat back ahead of you, you will find a useful book of information that you are welcome to take with you after the flight. Our in flight movie tonight is the classic "The Plane Crash." If you require a snack during your flight, feel free to munch on the thing next to you."

Matthew grabbed the book in the seatback ahead of him just as the engines roared to life and the creaking plane took off into the pitch black night. Matthew was so tired he could not keep his eyes open and in the darkness, fell asleep.

The crackling sound of the intercom woke Matthew. *"As you exit the plane, make sure to gather all of your belongings. Anything left behind will be eaten by the flight attendants."*

Matthews looked around and noticed no one on board. He looked at his watch which read one minute after midnight. He looked out of the window and saw his hometown airport.

His family was delighted to have their Daddy home early to enjoy Halloween. Matthew knew that no one would believe his story so he kept it to himself. He gave his youngest daughter the book he took from the seatback on the plane, its title; FUN CAMPFIRE STORIES.

He reflected back on the last announcement he heard as he exited the plane, *"Thank you for flying Halloween Airlines. We hope you enjoyed giving us the business as much as we enjoyed taking you for a ride."*

The luckiest man who did not know it

Once there was a man who lived in a beautiful home. He had everything but was never happy. The man believed it was because he was unlucky.

One day he had enough and he went to a very old and wise witch who lived in the swamp outside of town. The man wanted to find out why he was not lucky. The old and wise witch told him he must visit the oracle which was the source of all knowledge and ask it that question. *"Where do I find this oracle?"* The man asked. *"Travel to the west until you reach the end of the world and there you will find the oracle,"* said the old witch as she stirred her cauldron.

So the man set off to find the oracle at the end of the world and ask why he was not lucky. He walked for a day, he walked for a week, he walked for a month and he even walked for a year until he came to a clearing in the dark woods which was surrounded by werewolves.

One one side of the clearing were these strong and vicious looking werewolves. On the other side was a small, scrawny, sickly looking werewolf. The man decided to walk towards the scrawny werewolf. As he passed, the werewolf asked, *"Where are you going?"* *"I am going to visit the oracle and ask it why I have no luck,"* answered the man.

"Interesting, if you find it can you please ask it why I am not as strong and as vicious as my brothers," asked the werewolf. *"Of course,"* the man answered as he walked off.

He walked for a day, he walked for a week, he walked for a month, he even walked for a year until he got to a beautiful forest. The trees were vast and stretched far up into the sky, but in a small clearing was a short, leafless tree with spindly branches. As the man walked by, the little tree called out, *"Excuse me where are you going?"* *"I am going to the end of the world to visit the oracle and ask it why I have no luck.*"

"*Fascinating, if you find the oracle can you ask it why I am not as tall and strong as my brothers,*" the tree asked. "*Of course,*" answered the man as he walked off.

He walked for a day, he walked for a week, he walked for a month, and he even walked for a year until he came to a small pink house. Surrounding this cute house was a beautiful garden filled with bright flowers with vibrant colors. As the man was about to pass the house the most beautiful woman the man had ever seen came onto the front porch. The beautiful woman invited the man in for dinner. The man agreed and shortly he enjoyed a wonderful feast cooked to perfection by the beautiful woman. As they ate, the man told his story and at the end the woman asked, "*If you find the oracle can you ask it why I am so lonely?*"

"*Of course I can,*" answered the man. After dinner the man said his farewells to the beautiful woman and continued his journey to the west.

He walked for a day, he walked for a week, he walked for a month, he even walked for a year until finally he reached the end of the world. There, glowing on a column of pure gold was the oracle. The man called out, "*Excuse me. I have traveled a long way and endured many hardships to get here. Please tell me why I have no luck."* The oracle started to glow brighter and brighter suddenly a voice said, *"You have all the luck you need. It is all around you, you just don't notice it. Be more aware of your surroundings and you can find your luck."*

The man pondered the answer that the oracle had given him when he remembered the other questions that he had promised to ask the oracle. Just as he was about to ask, the oracle started to glow brighter and brighter and then a voice said, *"There is no need to ask the questions. I already know what they are, for I know everything."* The oracle than proceeded to answer all the questions that the man had promised to ask. The man thanked the oracle and then began his long journey home.

He walked for a day, he walked for a week, he walked for a month, he walked for a year when he arrived at the cute little pink house and knocked on the door. The beautiful woman was overjoyed to see him and after they enjoyed another fabulous meal, the man told the beautiful woman that the oracle had an answer for her.

"The oracle told me why you are so lonely. It said you must get married." *"Of course. Why didn't I think of that, it makes sense. Will you marry me?"* The beautiful woman asked the man.

"I am sorry," the man said. *"I can not marry you because I must find my luck first. But, the first nice man I see, I will send back to you."* With that he gave his farewells and continued heading east towards home.

He walked for a day, he walked for a week, he walked for a month, and he walked for a year until he reached the beautiful forest. The man saw the small tree and told it what the oracle said, *"The reason you are small and have no leaves is because buried beneath your roots is a chest full of gold. It is blocking your roots from receiving the nutrients you need to grow tall." "Of course, that makes sense. Please, some workmen left shovels over there. If you dig up the chest, you can keep the gold inside,"* said the little tree.

"I am sorry, I can not dig up the gold now because I must find my luck first. But the first strong man I see, I will send back to help you," the man said as he continued his journey home.

He walked for a day, he walked for a week, he walked for a month, and he even walked for a year until he reached the clearing in the dark woods where the werewolves lived. The scrawny werewolf walked up to the man and asked if he had gotten an answer to his question from the oracle. The man told the werewolf the whole story of his journey and then told him what the oracle said. *"The reason you are small and scrawny is because you do not eat enough. You must eat the first big stupid piece of meat you see."*

The werewolf thought that this made total sense and so he did.

The Nicren

There is a parallel dimension that is like ours, but also different. This dimension is called Htrae (which is earth in reverse). Htrae has a lot of real creatures that we consider in our dimension to be imaginary. Every once and a while, usually in an isolated spot like this, the two dimensions of Earth and Htrae intersect and a passageway is available between the two dimensions. Usually the opening is brief and nothing goes through the passage, but sometimes the dimension gateway is open longer and occasionally people, animals, birds and insects from our dimension pass through to Htrae. Likewise, sometimes things from Htrae pass through to our earth. This is why sometimes you hear stories of monsters, unicorns, ghouls, witches and all sorts of strange creatures having been spotted in our dimension.

Jennie and Lori had passed through one of these openings by accident a couple of days before. They were best friends heading out on a camping trip on a bright sunny Saturday. They were hiking a trail that they had hiked several times before and planned on staying a couple of nights in the woods. As they were heading down the trail the wind came up fast and then a bright flash of light. All of a sudden, Jennie and Lori found themselves on the same trail, but it was different. The plants were strange and there were two suns in the sky. The girls knew something had happened to them, but they had no idea what it was.

After a short distance down the trail, Jennie spotted a strange looking house across the field. It was almost rounded, like a half dome, made of wood and stone. The girls thought that they would stop there and try to find out where they were and what had happened to them.

The door to the house was short, only coming up to chin level on the girls. They knocked on the door. They heard the door unlock from the inside and then slowly open. Standing in the doorway was a little elf. He had long hair and a kind looking face with a big smile. He looked at the girls with an expression that seemed to say, I know who you are.

The girls started to tell the little man what had happened to them when, in the middle of the story, he interrupted and finished it for them. He explained that this was not the first time that some disoriented strangers had came down the trail and he knew that they had come through a doorway, a doorway that they could not go back through.

The girls looked at each other with a concerned look when in the distance came the sound of the most terrifying howl they had ever heard. Lori looked at the little elf and asked what that noise was. The little elf said that it was the howl of the Nicren. *"The Nicren,"* he said, *"are the most terrifying creatures in Htrae. They are very big, very strong, very fast, very ugly and eat any type of meat."* The elf pointed to a nearby hill and said that on the other side of the hill was a valley of large trees and on the other side of the valley was another hill. These monsters lived in the valley woods. He continued, *"There are two types of these monsters, one was called the Grizzle and the other type was known as the Grazzle and their both equally mean."*

The girls asked the elf how they could get home. The elf said, *"Well there is good news and bad news. The good news is that a passageway opens one day after the passageway you came through closes. The bad news is that the passageway is on the other side of the valley of tall trees...where the Nicren hunt."*

The girls got exact directions to the location of the other passageway and then asked the elf if he could tell them how to get around the Nicren. The little elf told the girls that there were some small bells that could help them, but they could find the bells and how to use them over at the building on the hill where the town hardware was sold. The girls thanked the little elf and headed toward the building on the hill.

As the girls entered the building they saw another little elf behind the counter. The clerk asked if he could help them. Jennie and Lori said that they had to go through the valley and they needed some bells to protect them from the Nicren. The clerk pointed to a shelf on the far side of the store. The girls went over and picked up two small tinker bells. As they came back to the counter they asked the clerk how the bells would protect them. The elf clerk said that the bells would only protect them from the Grizzle Nicren, but had no effect on the Grazzle. In order to get protection from the Grazzle they needed a special colored ribbon that was available next to the counter. The girls were about to buy two tinkle bells and two ribbons when the clerk said, *"You know that the tinkle bell and the ribbon cancel each other out so a person could only carry one item in order for it to work."* Lori decided to get the ribbon and Jennie bought the tinkle bell.

Lori asked the clerk how they would know if there were any Nicren around as they moved through the woods.

The clerk said, *"You can tell by their fresh droppings"*

The girls asked if there was a way to tell the difference between Grazzle droppings and Grizzle droppings.

"Sure," said the clerk. *"Grazzle droppings have tinker bells in them and the Grizzle droppings have a special color ribbon in them."*

The girls thanked the clerk, packed up their things and started the long walk through the valley woods.

The tall trees blocked a lot of sunlight reaching the forest floor so the woods took on a gloomy appearance. It was not long before the girls started seeing the remains of other animals that had fallen prey to the Nicren. As the sun set, the girls drew closer together as they tried to be as quiet as a mouse traveling through the darkening forest.

Soon they started seeing Nicren droppings. Some droppings had tinker bells and some with ribbons. As they walked on there were more and more of the droppings.

Suddenly, the girls heard the bushes moving, but there was no wind. It was too dark now to see far so the girls just hugged each other and remained silent. Soon the bushes were moving on all sides of them.

In the shadowy darkness the creatures moved in a circle around the frightened girls. They did not think they were going to survive the ordeal, so the only thing they could do was huddle together and hope that the tinkle bell and ribbon would somehow protect them.

(Now the Grizzles and the Grazzles were foul looking creatures. They stood 12 feet tall covered in very wiry, dirty hair with huge feet. The most remarkable feature about them was that they only had one eye. The Grazzle's eye was in the front of their head and the Grizzle's eye was located in the back of their head. They moved in pairs with a Grazzle walking in the front and a Grizzle walking behind the Grazzle. They never saw eye to eye and always seemed to argue.)

A howling growl broke the temporary silence. One part of the circle of creatures opened and through the dark mist there appeared a two headed monster larger than the others with hair that hung down to the ground. This beast had long blood stained claws and globs of goo rolling out from one corner of its fanged mouth.

The other creatures seemed to bow at the presence of this horrific beast. It walked up halfway between the other monsters and the girls. It looked at the girls with fiery red eyes for a full minute then suddenly spoke in a very rough voice, *"What are you?"*

The girls, in shock, responded, *"Human"*

"Pleased to eat you," the monster said. *"What are you doing here?"*

"We're just passing through your woods to get home." Jennie said.

"Where is home?" The creature asked.

"We come from another dimension, a place called earth." Lori responded.

"I see you have two heads and four eyes and do not have a lot of meat on you. Are there more of your type?" (Apparently, since the girls were huttled together, they appeared as one.) The girls thought for a minute then an idea popped into their heads, they whispered in each others ears. They had a plan.

While the girls were planning their next move, the creatures in the circle started to argue about how they were going to eat this trespasser into their woods. They had never encountered a creature that could repel both a Grizzle and a Grazzle.

All of a sudden Jennie and Lori yelled at the top of their lungs. The yell startled the creatures into silence. Jennie then said, *"We are skinny because we have not eaten in such a long time. Where we come from all the best food has been eaten and we have come to look for more. We have two heads because two heads are better than one and we have four eyes so we can see what we are eating and watch what will be eaten next."* As they said this, the girls stared at the creatures as hard and mean looking as possible.

The two headed Nicren looked bewildered at the girls and then asked, *"What is this best food of yours?"*

The girls turned their heads and body in unison so as to look at every creature encircling them. Then Jennie in a loud voice said, *"Our favorite food is Grizzle and Grazzle feet."* As Jennie said this they looked down at the creatures' feet and started to drool.

You could have cut the silence with a knife. The Grizzle tried to look at the Grazzle while they slowly started to back up. The two headed Nicren sheepishly said, *"You know that the feet of the one headed Nicren tastes a lot better than the feet of the two headed Nicren,"* as he too began to back up.

Suddenly, the girls yelled loudly and sprang together toward the two headed Nicren. You would not believe how fast that long haired, big footed creature could turn and run as it let out a terrified scream. At the site of this, the rest of the Nicren turned and ran into the dark mist just as fast as their big feet would allow.

The two girls snickered and gave each other a high five and continued on their journey through the woods, never seeing another Nicren.

Jennie and Lori found the passageway home the next day and they always went together whenever they went into the woods again.

FUN CAMPFIRE STORIES ANTHOLOGY

The long sales call

One morning, Mary Katherine, a door to door saleswoman of fine women's household products, knocked on Mr. Benson's door and asked if the lady of the house was in. Mr. Benson, a quiet man of few words, responded succinctly that his wife wasn't there.

"Well," continued Mary, *"Could I please wait for her return?"* Mr. Benson stated that he did not think his wife would be home anytime soon, but if she wanted to wait she was welcome to. Mr. Benson showed her into the living room and left her there for several hours.

Mary called out to Mr. Benson and asked him if he was able to call his wife to inquire as to when she would be home. Mr. Benson said that he was sure his wife would not answer the call.

The saleswoman began to feel a little worried so she called out to Mr. Benson and asked, *"May I know where your wife is?"*

"She went to the cemetery," he replied.

"Oh I'm sorry," said Mary, *"Was it somebody close to you?"*

"Yes very close," was Mr. Benson's response

"Did you go to the funeral?" Mary asked.

"Yes," said Mr. Benson.

"So you think your wife will be coming home soon?" asked Mary.

"I don't really know," Mr. Benson said and then he added.

"She's been there eleven years now."

Let's go fishing.

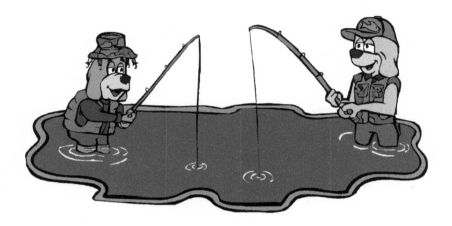

Planning a fishing trip in the wilds takes a lot of planning. Charlie and Leonard were amateurs when it came to camping and fishing, but there's a first time for everything. They spent months planning their two night adventure. They found a perfect spot in the pine treed bank along beautiful Carson Creek

They went to the outfitter's store and spent four thousand dollars buying sleeping bags, a tent, backpacks, cooking gear, fly rods, tackle, fishing vests and waders. They spent three hundred dollars each on out of state fishing licenses. They filled up the truck with gas, another fifty bucks, and spent two hundred more dollars on food, drink, flashlights and sun block.

Soon the day of departure arrived. It was a beautiful day as Charlie and Leonard packed the truck and headed down the road toward Carson Creek wilderness. About one hundred miles down the road the truck had a flat tire. Unfortunately, Leonard had taken the spare out to make room for all the gear. Charlie had to call a tow truck that cost one hundred dollars to tow the truck to the nearest shop. After getting a new tire mounted and buying a spare, the pair were set back another three hundred dollars.

It was late afternoon when Charlie and Leonard pulled the truck into the trailhead parking lot. They loaded up with their gear and started down the trail. Since they were behind schedule, it got dark quickly and the buddies found it harder to follow the trail at night. It started to rain and continued to rain on and off until morning when Charlie and Leonard, exhausted and wet, finally arrived at their campsite.

They spent the morning drying out their gear, setting up their tent and looking at the beautiful creek. Although they were tired, they looked forward to getting out in the creek right after they gathered some firewood and had lunch.

Charlie and Leonard went into the surrounding woods to gather firewood. Charlie got a big splinter in is right hand from an old log and Leonard received a bite from a spider he did not see under another log.

They were both famished since they had not eaten a bite since the day before so they planned on a big, hot lunch. Unfortunately, the wood was wet and so were the matches so the pair had to make do on a couple of cans of SPAM.

After lunch they put their waders and fishing vests on, grabbed their rods and stepped into the creek. Ok, things had not gone quite as planned up to this point, but it would be all good from this point forward, they thought.

The babbling creek was beautiful. The water was crystal clear as it flowed over smooth rocks. Thank goodness they had spent the extra money on insulated waders since the water was so cold. It took some time for Charlie and Leonard to get their casting skills refined enough to have a chance at success. Leonard was becoming self-assured as he told Charlie to, *"Watch this cast!"* Leonard drew back his rod and flicked his fly back, which lodged its hook into Charlie's waders. Upon executing a powerful forward thrust with his rod, the hook tore a seven inch long opening in the waders which promptly filled with near ice cold water.

Charlie fished from the bank the rest of the afternoon without success due to the fly constantly catching the trees. Leonard had equal luck on his continued attempts. It was late afternoon when the friends returned to their campsite. They soon discovered that an animal of some sort had discovered their food. There was little left except some crushed cans of SPAM.

Leonard started a fire, while Charlie decided to take one last cast from the bank before dark. There was a tug on the rod and the fight was on. Leonard cheered Charlie on as he reeled the monster in. After a hard fought battle, Charlie landed a rainbow trout that had to be close to four inches long. *"At least we have some real meat for dinner."* Charlie said.

Charlie and Leonard finished their dinner of SPAM and four bites each of fresh trout. Leonard didn't even mind the fishbone that pierced his cheek. Darkness engulfed the campsite except for the flickering flames of the fire as the stars shined brighter than the friends had ever seen. *"This is what it's all about,"* they said. Tomorrow they would take turns using the waders and rake them in.

Charlie and Leonard crawled into the tent and zipped up their sleeping bags for a good night's sleep. The owl in the tree over the tent was really loud, but heck it's the sound of nature. Speaking of nature, Leonard had the call of nature and had to relieve himself. Not thinking, he only went a foot or two outside the tent and peed on the small hill above the tent. The liquid ran down hill and saturated a nearby fire ant mound. The ants became aggravated and soon found the tent to attack. Their swarms soon found the entrance and with in a couple of minutes, Charlie and Leonard were yelling and jumping around the campsite in their underwear, swatting ants of their body parts. No going back to the tent that night, so the friends wrapped up in their ponchos and lay down on the hard ground next to the now nonexistent fire.

Even though they were exhausted, sleep was a commodity hard to come by that night. Their backs hurt from the hard ground, it was cold and the owl's hoots were not conducive to sleep.

As the sun rose the next morning, the sore, exhausted and hungry friends became determined to catch fish. Charlie's hand was throbbing from the splinter and the spider bite had caused a nasty bump on Leonard, but rainbow trout was on the menu. Since they had fished up creek the day before, they decided to go downstream. Charlie used the waders first while Leonard watched from the bank. At midday they switched. By the end of the day they were done. Not a single bite!

As they returned to their camp, they saw that the animal visitor from the day before had returned and took the rest of their food. All of the SPAM, that they thought to secure inside the tent, was gone and the tattered remnants of the tent stood as a testament to the short battle. The friends laid their rods by the bank as they surveyed the scene.

No food, no fish, no tent, thank God they were out of there in the morning. Leonard looked for the matches, but they were nowhere to be found. Clouds gathered and the rain began to fall. Charlie and Leonard huddled under their ponchos under the tall pine on the small hill overlooking the campsite. It got dark, it got cold and the rain got harder. Soon the friends watched as the swelling creek became a river and washed away their rods, backpacks and the rest of their gear.

Late the next morning, Charlie and Leonard made it back to the trailhead parking lot. What a welcome site, until the friends got close enough to the truck to discover the broken window and the missing radio and spare tire.

The trip home was quite except when the silence was broken by Charlie who said, *"Can you believe that we spent over five thousand dollars for one lousy undersized fish?"*

After a short pause, Leonard said, *"Thank goodness we only caught one!"*

The special one

S ara had studied hard and worked hard, but finally her day was here. She had always wanted to be a Doctor, not just any Doctor, but an animal Doctor. She was graduating Veterinary school and had been offered a job by the county. She graduated with honors and the next day showed up at the county offices.

Sara was briefed on her new responsibilities by the retiring Veterinarian, Dr. Russell. She learned that her responsibilities included making the rounds at the farms in the county once a week to assist the farmers as best she could.

Her first week on the job was mostly uneventful; the usual horse vaccinations, sprained dog paws, and sick cows. However, when she got to the Dudley farm, she saw something extraordinary.

While she was talking to farmer Dudley, a pig came ambling around the corner of the barn. What was extraordinary about it was that the pig had three artificial legs!

Sara asked farmer Dudley about this curious sight. Why would anybody give a pig even one artificial leg, much less three?

"Well," he drawled, *"that there ain't no ordinary pig. Let me tell you. One day I was out baling some hay, and I hopped off the tractor to check the tire, which was kind a wobbly. Wouldn't cha know it, the tractor started to roll of its own accord, and trapped me right there under the wheel. Just then old Pinky the pig wandered by and saw what happened. She skedaddled back to the house and fastened her teeth on my wife's apron and wouldn't let go until he dragged her out to where I was layin'. Luckily, my wife was able to get the tractor off me."*

Sara was quite impressed. She knew that pigs were pretty intelligent, but she had never heard of a pig doing anything like that. *"That's amazing,"* she said, *"But that still doesn't explain the artificial limbs."*

Dudley said. *"My son was down at the swimin' hole over yonder a couple summers ago. He hit his head on a big log out in the middle of the pond. He was about to go down for the third time, when old Pinky jumped into the water, swam out to him, grabbed him by the shorts with her teeth, and drug him coughing and spluttering up onto the bank. Saved my son's life, that pig did."*

"Incredible!" she exclaimed. *"Most pigs can't even swim! But the artificial legs...?"*

"Well, last year the old farmhouse burned down," Dudley continued. *"We were all asleep when the fire started, but old Pinky ran squealing around the house 'til we all woke up. She even went and dragged my youngest daughter from her bedroom just seconds before the roof collapsed."*

"That's one special pig," Sara said, *"but please, tell me, why does Pinky have three artificial legs?"*

"Well," said farmer Dudley, *"a pig like that's just too good to eat all at once."*

FUN CAMPFIRE STORIES ANTHOLOGY

The grizzly

Tim met Christopher when Christopher married Tim's sister. Being brother in laws, Christopher tried to get along with Tim and he was always tiring hard to find a common interest between himself and Tim. Tim, on the other hand, was braggadocios know it all.

One holiday, when the family was together Christopher mentioned that he would love to go hunting sometime. Tim said that he had hunted all sorts of game, but the most fun was bear hunting.

Tim bragged that he was so good at it that he could almost catch them with his bare hands and skin them.

On the way home from the family gathering, Christopher told his wife, who was Tim's sister, about what Tim had said. She told Christopher that Tim had never been bear hunting or any type of hunting before. She was sure that Tim had never even seen a real bear before except maybe at the zoo.

Christopher still thought that this might be an opportunity for Tim and him to bond, so Christopher rented a small one room shack in the middle of bear territory during bear season. Christopher called up Tim and invited him on the trip all expenses paid. Tim agreed to go.

When Tim and Christopher reached the isolated cabin in the middle of the woods, all Tim could do was complain, complain and complain some more. The cabin was too cramped he could have found a better place. There was no electricity, no television and no phone. He did not want to cook his own food. There was no indoor plumbing, and on and on. Christopher about had his fill, but decided to grin and bear it for the sake of peace.

The next morning, Christopher got up early, got a fire going, put on the coffee and scrambled some eggs for Tim and himself. He was looking forward to getting out in the woods for a chance to see a bear. Tim just complained about how early it was and the racket that Christopher was making.

Christopher said. *"Come on Tim, lets get out in the woods and do some bear hunting. It will be a lot of fun!"*

Tim said that he did not want to go. He could skin a bear with his bare hands he had hunted bear so many times. It was no longer a challenge, but a bore. As a matter of fact, he had decided to sleep in late get up, pack up and get out of that cheap cabin and head home later that morning.

Christopher had is fill of it. *"Suit yourself,"* he told Tim as he left the cabin with his rifle.

Christopher had barely made it one hundred yards down the trail when he spotted a bear cub walking across the path ahead of him. A slight grin formed on his face as he watched the cuddly cub walking through the underbrush apparently curious about everything, but oblivious to the presence of Christopher.

Suddenly and without warning, there came a horrendously loud and ferocious growl from the path ahead of him. Standing over seven feet tall on its hind legs, a grizzle bear was growling at Christopher. It was just a few dozen yards ahead, swiping the air with its huge front paws with razor sharp claws. The bear's jaws were crammed with teeth each looking like they were a foot long.

Christopher was frozen with fear as he gazed at the menacing creature. He had not expected anything like this. His legs were trembling, but otherwise would not move. The huge grizzle lowered its front paws to the ground making an audible thud as it thrust its massive body in a run toward Christopher. Christopher raised his rifle. Sweat was dripping down his forehead and the salt was stinging his eyes. His arms were trembling just as much as his legs. He would do anything to be anywhere else at that moment. The gun went off with a BANG! The noise shocked Christopher out of his petrified state. The bear rolled into the bushes, but within a moment, Christopher knew that he was still in big trouble. The bullet had barely grazed the giant beast on the left shoulder and it had regained its footing and charged towards Christopher, even madder than before.

Christopher pulled the trigger again, but the gun jammed. He threw the rifle at the charging ton of man killer as he turned and ran as fast as he could back towards the cabin. The bear caught the rifle in its mouth and snapped it in two like it was a toothpick.

The bear was gaining on Christopher. He was shouting at the top of his lungs for Tim to help him. As Christopher got closer to the cabin, all he could hear was the thud of bear claws right behind him and Tim yelling, *"Keep it quiet, I'm trying to get some sleep in here."*

Christopher reached the front step of the cabin and slipped, falling flat on his face. The grizzle bear was too close to stop. It tripped over Christopher and rolled through the front door of the cabin. Christopher jumped to his feet and closed the door to the cabin while he yelled out to Tim, *"You skin this one, and I'll get the next one!"*

Stars

Joe and Bill loved camping. It was their chance to get away from all the pressures of normal living. Out in the woods, they could relax and enjoy nature, instead of dwell in the constant headaches of the man made world they were forced to spend most of their time in. Out in the woods, it was all natural.

They hiked until they found an isolated spot deep in the forest. They set up their tent, rolled out their sleeping bags, gathered wood and started a fire.

After a filling dinner, they propped themselves on an old log and enjoyed the heat and light of the campfire as shadows danced off the canopy of trees.

Joe took out his book, FUN CAMPFIRE GHOST STORIES, and Joe and Bill took turns reading some of the stories out loud. This was the life! It was a peaceful, calm and beautiful night away from people, crime and problems.

The night wore on and the fire slowly burned down to a glowing mound of embers, when they crawled in their tent and fell sound asleep.

Some hours later, Joe woke up and stared at the night sky for several minutes. Joe reached over and shook his friend awake and said, *"Bill, look up at the sky and tell me what you see."*

Bill replied, *"I see millions of stars."*

"What does that tell you?" asked Joe.

Bill pondered the question for a minute and then he said, *"Astronomically speaking, it tells me that there are millions of galaxies, and potentially billions of planets.*

Astrologically, it tells me that Saturn is in Leo. Time wise, it appears to be approximately a quarter past three in the morning.

Theologically, it's evident the Lord is all-powerful and we are small and insignificant.

Meteorologically, it seems we will have a beautiful day tomorrow.

What does it tell you, Joe?"

Joe was silent for a moment, then said, *"Bill, you stupid moron, someone has stolen our tent."*

A letter from camp

S ometimes, the scary stuff is for the parents at home.

Dear Mom,

Our scout master told us all to write to our parents in case you saw the flood on TV and worried. We are OK. Only one of our tents and two sleeping bags got washed away. Luckily, none of us got drowned because we were all up on the mountain looking for Chad when it happened. Oh yes, please call Chad's mother and tell her he is OK. He can't write because of the cast. I got to ride in one of the search & rescue jeeps. It was neat. We never would have found him in the dark if it hadn't been for the lightning. Scoutmaster Webb got mad at Chad for going on a hike alone without telling anyone. Chad said he did tell him, but it was during the fire so he probably didn't hear him.

Did you know that if you put gas on a fire, the gas can will blow up? The wet wood still didn't burn, but one of our tents did along with some of our clothes. John is going to look weird until his hair grows back. We will be home on Saturday if Scoutmaster Webb gets the car fixed. It wasn't his fault about the wreck. The brakes worked OK when we left. Scoutmaster Webb said that a car that old you have to expect something to break down; that's probably why he can't get insurance on it. We think it's a neat car. He doesn't care if we get it dirty, and if it's hot, sometimes he lets us ride on the tailgate. It gets pretty hot with ten people in a car. He let us take turns riding in the trailer until the highway patrolman stopped and talked to us.

Scoutmaster Webb is a neat guy. Don't worry, he is a good driver. In fact, he is teaching Terry how to drive. But he only lets him drive on the mountain roads where there isn't any traffic. All we ever see up there are logging trucks. This morning all of the guys were diving off the rocks and swimming out in the lake. Scoutmaster Webb wouldn't let me because I can't swim and Chad was afraid he would sink because of his cast, so he let us take the canoe across the lake. It was great. You can still see some of the trees under the water from the flood. Scoutmaster Webb isn't crabby like some scoutmasters. He didn't even get mad about the life jackets. He has to spend a lot of time working on the car so we are trying not to cause him any trouble.

Guess what? We've all passed our first aid merit badges. When Dave dove in the lake and cut his arm, we got to see how a tourniquet works. Also Wade and I threw up. Scoutmaster Webb said it probably was just food poisoning from the leftover chicken. He said they got sick that way with the food they ate in prison. I'm so glad he got out and became our scoutmaster. He said he figured out how to get things done better while doing his time.

I have to go now. We are going into town to mail our letters and attend the gun and knife show.

Don't worry about anything. We are fine.

Love,
Cole

P.S. How long has it been since I had a tetanus shot?

BC

Mrs. Linderfelt was a lady who was rather old-fashioned, always quite delicate and elegant, especially in her language. She and her husband were planning a week long vacation in Florida, so she wrote to a particular campground asking for a reservation. She wanted to make sure the campground was fully equipped, but didn't quite know how to ask about the toilet facilities. She just couldn't bring herself to write the word "toilet" in her letter. After much deliberation, she finally came up with the old-fashioned term BATHROOM

COMMODE. But when she wrote that down she still thought she was being too forward. So she started all over again, rewrote the entire letter referring to the bathroom commode merely as the BC. She wrote, *"Does the campground have its own BC?"*

Well, the campground owner, Rick Smith wasn't old-fashioned at all and when he got the letter, he just couldn't figure out what the woman was talking about. That BC business really stumped him. After worrying about it for awhile, he showed the letter to several campers, but they couldn't imagine what the lady meant either. So Rick finally came to the conclusion that the lady must be asking about the local Baptist Church, so he sat down and wrote the following reply:

Dear Madam:

I regret very much the delay in answering your letter, but I now take pleasure in informing you that a BC is located nine miles north of the campground and is capable of seating 250 people at one time. I admit it is quite a distance away, if you are in the habit of going regularly, but no doubt you will be pleased to know that a great number of people take their lunches along and make a day of it. They usually arrive early and stay late. It is such a beautiful facility and the acoustics are marvelous...even the smallest sounds can be heard quite well by all. The last time my wife and I went was six years ago, and it was so crowded we had to

stand up the whole time we were there. It may interest you to know that right now a supper is planned to raise money to buy more seats. They are going to hold it in the basement of the BC. I would like to say it pains me very much not to be able to go more regularly, but it surely is no lack of desire on my part. As we grow old, it seems to be more of an effort, particularly in cold weather. If you do decide to come down to our campground, perhaps I could go with you the first time, sit with you and introduce you to all the other folks. Remember, this is a friendly community.
Sincerely, Rick Smith

Deathbed

Peter was a well known music composer. Later in life, he had written seven musical ballads that had been well received by the community. He stopped composing when he fell sick. Peter had been very sick for a long time. The Doctor had long since said that he had done all that could be done. Peter was not long for this world, but it seemed that people where waiting for and almost wanting his demise.

"No...that could not be, you say?"

Well, how about the other day when the doorbell rang and Marcie, his wife, answered the door. Peter was sick, but he could still hear what was going on. Mr. Humphries was at the door. He was the local undertaker and gravedigger. Marcie asked Mr. Humphries how he was doing and he said, *"Very poorly, very poorly. I haven't buried a living soul in the past six weeks. Oh, by the way, how is Peter doing?"* Marcie responded that Peter was expected to go any hour now.

Later that day, Peter smelled the unmistakable aroma of fresh baked chocolate chip cookies. Peter was near death, but chocolate chip cookies were his favorite. He summoned the energy to climb out of bed and slowly made his way to the kitchen where his faithful wife was baking his most favorite treat. He spotted some cookies fresh out of the oven on the counter. He moved toward the counter and put out his hand to pick up a warm, delicious cookie. Suddenly, Marcie slapped his hand with the spatula and said, *"Don't touch them. They are for the funeral."*

Depressed, he made his way back to bed and died.

A popular man, Peter left Marcie strict instructions in his will for his wake to be a jolly and happy affair: a celebration of his life. To this end, Peter had left $52,000 dollars in his will for the party.

As the guests left at the end of the wake, Marcie was asked by her close friend, Alicia, if she thought that Peter would have been pleased. *"Well, I'm sure Peter would have been delighted,"* Marcie murmured.

"I'm sure you're right," replied her friend, Alicia, who lowered her voice and leaned in close. *"How much did all this really cost?"*

"All of it," Marcie said, *"Every penny of the $52,000 dollars."*

"What!" exclaimed Alicia in a higher than normal voice, *"I mean, it was very nice, but $52,000 dollars?"*

Marcia took a deep breath and answered, *"Look, Alicia, let me explain: the funeral cost $15,500. I donated $1,500 to the church. The wake, food and drinks were another $5,500. The rest went on the memorial stone."*

Alicia worked out the math in her head, *"Eh?"* she exploded for a second time, *"$29,500 for a memorial stone? My goodness, how big is it?"*

Marcie shows Alicia her ring finger, *"Oh about 30 carats,"* she smiled.

Later that week, there were reports of music coming from the graveyard. After an hour they were able to narrow down where it was coming from. It appeared that the music was coming from Peter's grave. Marcie and her friends, along with a slew of curious bystanders, stood next to Peter's gravesite and listened to the music. Marcie soon recognized the music as Peter's ballads except they were being played in reverse. This was a complete mystery until the undertaker, Mr. Humphries, arrived. He explained that Peter was just decomposing.

I'm not who you think I am

In high school, I needed money. I was able to drive, had a girlfriend, and liked to go out with my friends. My folks didn't have much money and I needed to pay my own way. I had worked at restaurants and grocery stores and wanted to try something more interesting. While searching around, I stopped at the zoo.

As it turned out, the zoo director liked my style and said he had an interesting job that he felt I could handle. We walked through the back alleys and tunnels of the zoo that most people never see until we got to the gorilla cage, but it was empty.

The director told me that their gorilla, named Kong, had caught a bug and was in quarantine for the next week. Kong was getting old and they were, even now, shopping around for a replacement. Kong just sits on a tree branch holding onto a rope all day. When the crowds started arriving on the weekend, they'd be disappointed to have no gorilla since everyone enjoys the gorilla exhibit, even a boring old gorilla.

The director said he had a gorilla suit I could wear if I would be interested in sitting on the branch for four hours at a time so the people would have something to look at. It sounded good to me, not the usual high school job, so I told him I would.

The next day I went to the zoo, put on the gorilla suit and climbed into the cage. I sat on the branch holding the rope and soon there was a crowd of children pressing their faces to the bars.

It didn't take long for me to start getting bored, so I started to scratch my armpits, thump my chest, and twirled the rope. About an hour passed and I began to really get into this gorilla thing. I would grab the rope and swing across the cage. The kids thought it was great so I started swinging higher and higher.

In the next cage there was a lion and he was becoming irritated by my antics. He began to pace in his cage and roar. I kept swinging and started to swing to the lion's side of the cage. I would use my feet to push off of his bars. As I swung out farther, he would roar even louder. It was, actually, a lot of fun and the kids were really enjoying the show.

All of a sudden, I missed the bars, flew through them and dropped right into the lion's cage! I landed on my back and was stunned, but immediately got up and ran to the front of the cage where the crowd was.

"Help me, help me, I'm not who you think I am!" I screamed.

Just as I yelled, the lion jumped on my back and knocked me to the ground. His head was at my neck and I was sure I'd never make it to graduation.

Then he whispered in my ear, *"Shut up stupid, or you'll get us both fired."*

FUN CAMPFIRE STORIES ANTHOLOGY

Things aren't always as they seem.

O nce upon a time, there was a very poor farmer that was down on his luck. He had sold off most of his livestock to pay his property taxes and soon had to resort to selling parts of his property.

One day, the tax collector came to the farmer and told him that if he gave him the two acres to the south that bordered the new high end subdivision, he would delay collecting the farmer's taxes for one year. The tax collector said that he was going to build an expensive house on the old foundation that was there. The farmer did not want to give away the property, especially since it was the location of the old family house that had burned down during the civil war, but he had little choice.

The tax collector was a selfish, greedy man. He knew that the farmer would not be able to pay is taxes now or in the future and he would be able to get all the property for a steal. The farmer agreed, but with one stipulation; that if the tax collector abandoned the property before the next tax bill was payable, it would revert back to him.

Within six months the ruthless tax collector had built a beautiful new mansion on the foundation of the farmer's old homestead.

Two traveling angels stopped to spend the night in the home of the tax collector. The tax collector's family was rude and refused to let the angels stay in the mansion's guest room. Instead, the angels were given a small space in the cold basement. As they made their bed on the hard floor, the older angel saw a hole in the wall and repaired it. When the younger angel asked why, the older angel replied, *"Things aren't always as they seem."*

The next night the pair came to rest at the house of the very poor, but very hospitable farmer and his wife. After sharing what little food they had, the couple let the angels sleep in their bed where they could have a good night's rest.

When the sun came up the next morning, the angels found the farmer and his wife in tears. Their only cow, whose milk had been their sole income, lay dead in the field.

The younger angel was infuriated and asked the older angel, *"How could you have let this happen? The first man had everything, yet you helped him. The second family had little, but was willing to share everything and you let their cow die."*

"Things aren't always as they seem," the older angel replied. *"When we stayed in the basement of the mansion, I noticed there was gold stored in that hole in the wall. Since the owner was so obsessed with greed and unwilling to share his good fortune, I sealed the wall so he wouldn't find it."*

"Then last night, as we slept in the farmer's bed during that terrible thunderstorm, the angel of death came for his wife. I gave him the cow instead. Lightning struck the tax collector's house and it burnt down to the foundation. The heat cracked the foundation wall exposing the gold within, which now belongs to the farmer and his wife. Things aren't always as they seem."

About the Author

John Bradshaw is a graduate of Furman University, former
United States Army Officer, former State of South Carolina
SITCON member, licensed private pilot, Black Belt in Karate
and business owner.
He is married to Alicia and they have three boys, Adam,
Christopher and Spencer
Visit John's website at www.eaglewingsbradshaw.com

Other published works:
FUN CAMPFIRE GHOST STORIES
FUN CAMPFIRE STORIES

CPSIA information can be obtained
at www.ICGtesting.com
Printed in the USA
FSHW01n2016071018
52836FS